THE SYNDICATE
VOLUME THREE

VOICES
Book Five
A.L. Kessler

LOST IT ALL
Book Six
Mia Bishop

VOICES

A.L. Kessler

CHAPTER ONE

"Come here little vampire."

The female voice coaxed Lisa Thorne to lift her head. She knew the voice well. It was the only living voice she ever heard, and it belonged to her handler.

A ghost sat by the door, her arms crossed. "Oh, yes little vampire, listen to the agent." The woman had been a witch. Trapped by the agency, away from the moon and starved of her from her magic, she had died.

Lisa glared at Rosella. "If I listen to her, she'll take me to feed." She gasped out, "I'm so hungry." She wrapped her arms around her stomach as it growled and twisted in pain.

"Come here, crazy girl," the woman said again, this time grabbing Lisa's hair and dragging her towards the black door that led to the dim hallway.

Lisa scrambled against the pain. "No, no, I don't want to leave. The voices," she cried out trying to scramble back, but the woman kept a grip on her hair.

"Come on."

Lisa didn't have the strength to fight her. The moment she was pulled out of the isolation room the voices of spirits assaulted her. They all tended to leave her alone inside the isolation chamber, but any time she left they yelled at her to listen to them. She threw her hands over her ears, shaking her head. God, they needed to stop screaming at her. All of them screaming over each other, begging for someone to speak out against the horrors of the Agency.

And being blood-starved made it that much worse. "Please, please let me feed first."

"After you tell us what happened at the drug warehouse."

Lisa shook her head. "No, no, no."

The woman bound Lisa's hands behind her back with silver cuffs, then shoved her forward. Lisa stumbled through the hallway with the woman at her back. Voices from the other rooms cried out to be set free, for their torture to stop. She couldn't tell which were physical and which were spirits. Her head pounded from the noises; the cramps in her stomach had her hunched over as she stumbled through the hall, trying to tell the spirits to hush. The woman shoved her into an elevator and punched a button. The car began to rise, shaking as it did, and then stopping.

The doors opened with a shudder, and Lisa was shoved forward. Her bare feet met the harsh asphalt, making her cringe.

She raised her eyes up and noted the black SUV in front of them, the engine running and the door open and waiting. Her handler shoved her forward. She hadn't been in a car since they took her to the scene of an explosion, but she had no way of telling how long ago that had been. She scrambled up into the vehicle with her handler behind her.

Lisa closed her eyes as the car started moving. The silver weakened her, so even if she weren't blood-starved, she wouldn't be able to escape. She pulled her knees up to her chest as pain shot through her stomach.

"Don't worry Lisa; you'll be able to feed after you do this for us."

It was a common promise when she went on trips like this. "Romulus promised that he would find a vampire to teach me about what I've become."

"Once he's sure you're not...crazy." The handler patted Lisa's head, and Lisa resisted the urge to bite her. At the thought of blood, Lisa's lips turned up exposing her fangs. A little bit of blood would satisfy her long enough until she could get her real meal from Romulus.

"I have the silver nitrate spray, don't make me use it on you again."

Lisa flinched back. "Maybe you should feed me more often, so I'm not starving all the time." Maybe that would help with all the voices.

"If I had it my way, you'd be shot with a silver bullet or left out to die in the sun. But Romulus seems to think you're sane enough for me to drag you out." She shook her head. "I think you just happened to work for the Syndicate before you were changed."

Lisa leaned her head against the window. "I don't even know who the Syndicate is. I don't even know where I am or who you people are."

"And I think you're lying."

With that, Lisa closed her eyes again and ignored the woman next to her.

The car came to a screeching halt, and Lisa's entire body tensed before her handler grabbed her hair and pulled her out. Lisa stumbled, almost falling out onto the ground. The moon cast a dark shadow from the warehouse on the ground. Her stomach churned as her handler opened the door and shoved her in. "Okay, tell me what you see."

Lisa looked around, her eyes wide as she saw the ghost of a man standing there with his hand shoved in his pocket. A gaping hole in the middle of his chest told her a little about how he died.

"Who are you?" she asked, well aware that her handler was rolling her eyes.

The ghost looked at her with wide eyes. "A medium vampire. Now that's new, even for the Agency." He flicked the plastic badge hanging from his shirt. "Agent Kershaw, now a ghost doomed to relive my last moments and trapped in limbo."

She glanced around for a death scene getting ready to play out. Some ghosts were forced to relive their death over again and again, and they were well aware they were stuck. Occasionally they could wander, normally following the person they loved.

The ghostly man in front of her started to shift into a wolf, and she backed up, stumbling over her feet. She landed on the ground as two blurry figures appeared and one slammed its hand into Kershaw's chest. Kershaw looked at her. "Syndicate bastard. Zeek." The images faded, and suddenly Kershaw was standing right back where he was before, just staring at her.

"What the hell are you babbling about?" Her handler grabbed her arm and yanked her up from the ground.

Kershaw smirked. "Oh, Tara is assigned to you. She's a great handler; I'm sure she's keeping you wrapped around her finger."

Tara. Lisa glanced up at the woman. "Tara," she muttered, never having heard the name until now.

"What did you see?" she snarled.

"A Syndicate member named Zeek killed Agent Kershaw," she muttered. "There was another figure there, but I don't know who; they are living or they didn't die here, so their souls and impressions aren't clear."

A wicked smile curved over Tara's lips. "Perfect. Let's go, that's all I need."

"Please, take me to feed. I gave you what you wanted." Her stomach cramped with pain. "I need his blood."

Tara smoothed Lisa's hair out almost as if she were a dog. "I'll take you to Romulus to feed after we have a little pit stop. I have to check on something."

Lisa couldn't decide if she was being strung along or not. Normally when they pulled her out of isolation, it was feed, then right back to the darkness. There were no other stops. No passing go, no collecting two hundred dollars. Tara grabbed her by the cuffs and shoved her back to the car.

They got in, and the driver left without any directions. "You're to stay in the car; you disobey me, and I will not take you to Romulus to feed. Understood?"

Lisa nodded. "Yes." She pulled her knees up again, trying to stop the hunger pains in her stomach. What were a couple more hours compared to the days she'd already gone without feeding?

The warehouses disappeared, and soon she could see the docks. Her heart leaped a little bit at seeing the openness of the water, a stark contrast between the claustrophobic feeling of the city and the isolation chamber. Huge shipping containers were laid out nearby, people walking around them holding firearms.

Her heart fell as she started to see glimpses of ghosts also wandering around. What was going on here? The images moved in and out of the containers as if being filed in. The car stopped a few yards from one, and Lisa had to control herself from pressing against the window to see more. At least ten ghosts were walking around the shipping yard.

Tara got out and looked over her shoulder. "Stay here."

Lisa gave a shaky nod, but didn't look at the woman; she was too focused on the ghosts in front of her. The car door shut and she watched as Tara and the driver approached one of the armed men.

He tugged on his bulletproof vest, showing the same badge that Lisa had seen on Agent Kershaw. So this was the Agency that was using her. They were up to something evil in the shipping yard.

"Oh, hello there."

Lisa let out a squeak and jumped, nearly hitting her head on the car's roof. In the seat next to her sat a woman no older than twenty, her body was slightly opaque, and her skin had a bluish tint to it. Most ghosts were just a see-through colored version of themselves, but this woman was bit different. "How did you die?"

"I suffocated. Couldn't breathe because I had an allergic reaction to a drug they'd given me." She patted the seat. "Right here, that evil woman dosed me up and led me to there." She pointed to the container. "Before the drug took effect, then left me in there with a bunch of other people."

Ghosts didn't normally lie, but that sounded far-fetched. "What kind of drug?"

"One made from scorpion venom, from what I understand. Or some form of it. You need to tell Remus about this. He has a special interest in a woman named Malia."

She snorted. "And why do you think that? I don't even know who Remus is." She wrapped her arms around herself. The smell of blood drifted in the air, and her stomach cramped. She looked up to see a guard across the way examining his hand. Her eyes locked on the bright red substance dripping over his fingers.

"Listen to me child, we ghosts talk. Find Remus with the Syndicate, tell him the name."

The voice faded away, and Lisa realized that it was because she wasn't in the car anymore. She was now standing in front of the guard who was holding his bleeding hand. She gave a twisted smile as he looked at her in fear. "I'm hungry." With speed she didn't realize she had, she went to strike.

Voices all around her started screaming, and she crashed to her knees, demanding that the voices shut up. She pulled against the cuffs behind her, but they wouldn't budge. All she wanted to do was cover her ears to keep the ghosts from yelling at her. They all screamed the same thing about finding Remus and telling him about Malia.

Tara came to her and yanked her off the ground. "I don't know how you managed to use your abilities with those cuffs on, but I told you to stay in the car."

"I'm so hungry," she whispered. "I can't block them out. The voices." She looked up at Tara, and the woman's eyes widened.

"Blood-starved."

No shit she was blood-starved; she hadn't fed recently. Tara led her back to the quiet of the car where the ghost from before was sitting in the middle seat now. "Make sure you tell Tara hi from her sister."

Lisa wasn't sure what came over her, but she tilted her head and looked straight at Tara. "Your sister says hi, you murdering bitch."

Tara back-handed her and Lisa's head snapped to the side.

Agency bastards. Alika crouched behind one of the shipping containers. He could hear people inside screaming out, thanks to his vampire hearing, but there was something more. He could sense another vampire around. He dodged behind a tower of boxes to take him closer to the car that just pulled up.

A woman and the driver got out of the car leaving someone else inside. He watched through the back window as the person seemed to be having a conversation with themselves, before turning his eyes away from them and to the lady and man who had gotten out of the car.

"The humans that are test subjects are being cleaned out with each new dose; I have the records here for how many doses it takes and withdrawal symptoms. Soon we'll be able to sort out which humans will be for sale and which won't fetch a profit."

Alika's heart fell. Humans in shipping containers and there wasn't anything he could do. He couldn't take on the number of Agency members that were walking around the dock. He might be able to come back later or have someone come back during daylight hours, but right now he just needed to gather information.

"Good, make sure you keep track of how many we lose. We need an idea of how strong the drug is with different variables."

She handed the guard a clipboard. "We'll start distributing the human product as soon as the trials are over. This is a list of who our next test subjects should be."

The guard scanned the paper. "Doable."

A grunt sounded through the area followed by the smell of blood. Alika grinned at the thought of fresh blood, but he needed to make sure that he kept his instincts under control. He saw another guard pull his hand away from a shipping container, cradling the bleeding palm. He licked his lips as the blood caught the moonlight.

A blur shot across the area and stopped in front of the bleeding guard. The vampire Alika had sensed, but something was wrong. "I'm hungry." Her limbs jerked, and she reared her head back to strike.

"Shut up," she whispered before crashing to her knees. The silver cuffs around her wrists caught his attention as she tried to pull them. She doubled over as if in pain, screaming 'shut up.'

He started to step up to help her but stopped. She was an agency hostage, which meant that she was important to them for some reason. They wouldn't let him just walk off with a hungry vampire. The woman who'd first gotten out of the car went and grabbed the vampire by the cuffs and snarled something in the woman's ear.

From his vantage point, Alika couldn't hear the exact words, but he took a moment to examine the vampire. Her long dark hair was unkept, tangled at the ends, clothes torn and ragged. She hunched over as she was forced back to the car, making her petite frame seem fragile. What the hell had happened to the poor woman? He wanted to rip her from the agent's grip and comfort her.

The thought struck him as odd. He hadn't wanted to care for anyone like that…since his family had been slaughtered. He rubbed his chest at the sudden reminder of grief.

The car drove off, and he slinked away. He had a report to fill out for Remus and Zeek, he'd make mention of the woman, and the boss would make a call on what to do about her.

The drive seemed to take forever. The crunching of the tires against the asphalt made Lisa cringe with each rotation. All she wanted to do was eat. That was it. After her last comment to Tara she didn't think she'd get to feed, but when the car finally stopped, she looked up at a huge house.

"This is where Romulus lives?" she asked without thinking.

Tara laughed. "No, this is where he is tonight, there's some sort of celebration going on. We'll get you fed and then back to isolation you go."

Lisa licked her lips. "Romulus will feed me? Promise me?"

"I can't promise you because it's up to him." Tara got out of the car and dragged Lisa out by the cuffs.

Lisa hissed as the metal dug in and burnt the skin of her wrists. She tried to keep her feet under her but stumbled. Tara knocked on the door of the massive home. The faux rock siding had vines crawling up the side, vacant of any leaves on both sides of the door.

The door opened, and woman with blond hair down to her knees stood there. "Oh Tara, Romulus wasn't expecting you tonight."

"I need to talk to him about the dock, and this thing," she jerked Lisa forward, "needs to feed."

The woman met Lisa's gaze with warm brown eyes. "She seems to need a lot more than feeding. Why don't you let me wash her up, you know Romulus won't want to touch her with how nasty she is now."

It was the first gesture of kindness anyone had shown in a while. She mentally begged that Tara would say yes.

"You have a point, but you are too kind Cassandra."

"Please, I insist. Besides, it gives Romulus a chance to excuse himself from the party. Let me get her settled, and I will send another servant down to fetch you and him when she is ready."

Tara bowed her head. "I'll go join the party." She tossed Lisa at Cassandra's feet.

The woman bent down and stroked her hair. "You poor dear," she whispered. "Blood-starved and lost. Come on." She helped Lisa stand and then led her down a dim passage.

"I'll take you to the servants' quarters to wash up." She waved a hand over the cuffs, and they fell to the ground. "Romulus and his people are such brutes. Where have they been keeping you? A cave?"

Lisa held her head in shame. "Isolation at some place called the Agency."

The woman stiffened. "They are trying to keep you hidden then. Or trying to break you. I've been with Romulus for years, and I've seen all manner of creatures go into isolation."

"Why would you stay with such an evil man?"

Cassandra shook her head. "I don't have a choice, but that's not the point here. Let's get you cleaned up. You're innocent; I can see that in your soul." She stroked Lisa's matted hair. "I'm going to get you out of Romulus' control."

Lisa shook her head. "I have nowhere to go; I'm a vampire. My family…I don't even know how long I've been gone at this point."

"I'm going to turn you over to a vampire who can get you some help. After you feed, you'll go back with Tara, just trust me." She pulled her into a bathroom. "If I could get you out now, I would, but Tara would become suspicious, and then I'd face Romulus' wrath."

Lisa tilted her head to the side. She had no doubt the man could cause some damage, but the tone made it seem like so much worse than a beating. "What is he?" She'd heard whispers through the ghosts, but even in death people were scared to speak of Romulus.

"You know the answer in your heart, Lisa." Cassandra gave her a knowing look. "You need help to teach you how to be a vampire and not a tool of the Agency."

"Agency, Syndicate, these words mean nothing to me." She shook her head. "This is my life now." Her heart broke at the words as she realized she'd given up hope on ever seeing the outside world again.

"You'll see," Cassandra promised. "Now, let's get you into a warm bath, washed, and into some fresh clothes."

Lisa peeked into the room and saw a large tub filled to the brim with steaming water. She slowly walked up to it and dipped her hand in. The water rippled and started to spill over the edge.

"Go on, it's a bathroom; the floor is meant to get wet."

Lisa stepped in and laid down, letting the warm water enclose her.

"Soaps and oils are on the table to your left, take your time, I'll find you some clothes."

The woman left, and Lisa found herself wondering what the woman was.

Alika exited Remus' office. The man was little more agitated than usual tonight. Normally he was the epitome of calm and collected. Alika sensed a different power from the man, but he didn't push. He wasn't far enough up on the totem pool to question Remus, just to report to him when Zeek told him to.

Speaking of Zeek, he was probably out screwing his mate. Getting a decent meal, while Alika was slumming around the streets. He could get a decent meal if he wanted, but he felt like he was betraying his love by feeding from someone else. Even if she was gone and she'd died before he'd become a vampire.

His phone rang, and he looked down at the number. Not one he knew, but since he didn't give his number to many people, he assumed it was friendly. "Speak," he barked as he walked down the hallway to the elevator.

"Alika, how nice to see that you're still so demanding."

His breath caught at the familiar voice. "Cassy? I haven't heard from you since…"

"Romulus invaded your village and you became a vampire, I know. You must listen to me now."

He could hear the begging in her voice. "You still work for him, how do I know I can trust you?"

"You can't, but you're going to want to. The fate of this stupid feud rests in the hands of a vampire that Romulus has."

His mind went to the vampire he'd seen earlier that night. "What are you talking about?"

"The woman has a special ability. Combined with my seer abilities and Romulus' influences she could make him unstoppable."

He didn't want to believe her. "That's not possible."

"The vampire is a medium, Alika," she snapped. "Do you want that in Romulus' hands? He's taken precautions to make sure that she stays with him; he controls her completely. Which means she is incapable of withholding information."

He growled. "What the hell do you want me to do about it then? He probably keeps her close to him if she's that important."

"No, she's kept in isolation." Her voice softened a little, "Kept like an animal, Alika."

He took a deep breath. "I have someone who might be able to get in there, but that's the best I can do. Remus isn't going to like the risky operation, but we'll snag her and get out, from there on she's on her own."

"I have a feeling you might change your mind. I have to go." She hesitated slightly. "For what it's worth Alika, I'm sorry."

He snorted. "Sorry doesn't bring them back, Cassy." He disconnected the call and sent a group text to the two people he knew could get someone out of isolation: Peterson and Skye. Between the two of them, they could get her out undetected. So he hoped. If he could convince Zeek that it was worth it, then he'd let Skye do the mission. This was going to go beyond simply erasing security footage.

He rode the elevator down and closed his eyes. He could see the long black hair of his love, her heart-shaped face, and sharp hazel eyes. Her creamy skin had been so soft beneath his touch when he'd come home from war. A petty squabble between villages that could have been stopped, but he had to take his troops there. That was before the slaughter.

Cassy had warned him about the attack by messenger. He'd befriend her while his troops stayed in one of the villages ruled by Romulus. He shook his head; he didn't want to think about it. He pushed the images of his wife out of his mind and stepped out of the elevator.

If there were one good thing this mission would do, it would be taking something priceless away from Romulus and giving it to Remus. One thing to help tip the scale and a chip in the revenge Alika wanted.

Lisa looked down at the jeans and t-shirt she now wore. It was strange not be in her torn-up clothes from before, and clean. She didn't smell like death anymore. Instead, she smelt like citrus and was scrubbed clean.

But she knew it wouldn't last. After she fed, she'd go back to her pit. In a way, the kindness shown was more torture, and she wondered if that was the point.

Cassandra came back in the room. "I let Romulus and Tara know that you are ready."

"Thank you." She followed Cassandra down the hallway and felt a little bit like she was being led to the slaughter. Her stomach cramped in anticipation of a long-awaited meal, and yet she knew that she'd get just enough to be satisfied, leaving her with an intense craving and want for more.

Cassandra opened the door at the end of the hall, and Lisa walked in, keeping her eyes down. "Thank you for seeing me."

"Tara said you provided her with decent information tonight. Told us what happened to one of my special agents." His smooth voice rolled over her, and she glanced up at him. His silver hair was pulled back away from his face. His eyes swirled with a power she'd never get used to.

He stepped up to her and put a finger under her chin. "Do you know if the shifter lived?"

"I can tell you that they..." she hesitated at how to put it. "That I wasn't able to see them there."

He hmmed and stepped away from her. "That's not an answer."

"The best I can assume is yes, but I can't promise it. If she died somewhere else, I wouldn't know it from that one scene." She tried not to panic.

He turned his back to her. "Tara will take you there tomorrow, where they said she died."

She realized he wasn't going to feed her. Panic flooded through her "I need blood. Please." She took a step toward him.

He spun around, and she stopped in her tracks. "You will feed tomorrow when you give me the information I need."

Her heart fell, and she failed to find any words to respond. She looked back to see if Cassandra was there to back her up, but the woman was gone. Her eyes darted to Tara, begging her.

"You heard him, bloodsucker." Lisa twirled her finger. "Turn around so I can cuff you."

A wicked smile crossed Lisa's face; she wasn't cuffed. That's right. She demanded her body take her to Romulus, and to her surprise, it worked. She was standing in front of him, reaching for his wrist to bite, but he threw his hand up, and something hit her. An invisible barrier shoved her to the ground.

She cried out and tried again, but Romulus wrapped his hand around her throat. She clawed at his hands, her body still panicking at the lack of air even though she was dead.

"Have you not heard the phrase, don't bite the hand that feeds you?"

"I am hungry. Starving me isn't going to get you the information any faster." She dropped her hands to her side. "It impairs my abilities to think of anything else but blood."

He tossed her to Tara who wasted no time getting the cuffs on. "My decision still holds, especially after that little stunt."

She hung her had again and didn't fight Tara as she started to walk out. Back to isolation, back to the dark, damp room, with only the ghosts to keep her company. She could run, but there was no doubt in her mind that Romulus would find her and drag her back. The information she provided was too valuable to him.

CHAPTER TWO

Lisa wasn't sure how much time had gone by, but she was sure that Tara hadn't taken her out to the scene right away on purpose. To draw out the time between feedings even further. She closed her eyes against the images that flashed in front of her. Illusions often came when she felt the full force of bloodlust, and they mixed with the ghosts she already saw until she wasn't sure what was real and what wasn't. She curled up in the corner of her chamber, pulling her knees to her chest.

Rosella's soft voice sang an old lullaby to her while the ghost stroked her hair, a bit of comfort in the pain. A shrill noise went through the building, and Lisa threw her hands over her ears. What the hell?

The increased sensitivity of being a vampire made the noise pierce through her brain, giving her an instant migraine to join the hunger pains. She looked at Rosella. "What's going on?"

"I'll check if I can." The ghost faded away, and Lisa waited with her hands covering her ears.

The door popped open, and Lisa lifted her head from her knees. No one peeked in, no one called. She stood and pushed it open just a little bit further and looked down the hall. A man stood there...no, not a man, another vampire.

His shoulder length dirty blond hair was pulled back at the base of his neck, and his blue eyes pierced her gaze. Behind him stood the shadow of three people, but they weren't clear enough to make out. She tilted her head slightly at the strange apparitions. "You must be Lisa. Come on; we don't have a lot of time."

She looked around for Rosella or for any clue that this wasn't an illusion caused by the bloodlust but found nothing.

"Come on; I don't have time to waste on you." He rushed forward and grabbed her arm. She tried not to cringe as he pulled her towards a different elevator. Tara lay on the floor to the left, and Lisa gasped.

He used a badge to call the elevator down and then tossed it on the floor where Tara's body was.

"She's not dead," he said without her asking the question. "I knocked her out so that she couldn't stop you from coming to me."

"She wouldn't have been able to stop you; you're a vampire, she's not." She didn't move her gaze from the body until the doors shut. "Who are you?"

He smirked. "I'm under strict orders not to kill anyone while I'm on Agency grounds. I'm Alika, Cassy called me a few weeks ago to get you out of this hellhole."

Cassy? "Cassandra?" she asked softly.

He nodded. "It's taken us that long to arrange this so don't blow it. As soon as we're able to, I want you to transport yourself back to wherever you came from. Go back to your life."

What he was saying didn't make any sense to her. She shook her head. "I don't really know how to do that. I can't go back home."

The shrill noise stopped, and she looked at him in panic. "Please don't let them take me back there."

He cursed. "New plan, as soon as I can, I'll take us somewhere."

"What do you mean as soon as you can. Why can't we go now?" Her voice rose a bit in panic.

"Because there's a special spell on the building that keeps vampires from doing that. Stay close to me." He wrapped his fingers around her wrist again just as the doors opened.

She glanced around at the empty building. "What happened? Shouldn't there be people up here?"

"The fire alarm went off, and everyone left. Then I had the security system put the building into lockdown, but Skye was only able to keep it in lockdown for a little bit, so it won't be long until people get back in." He took her to the back emergency exit and put his hand on the door, waiting.

She was going to ask who Skye was but wanted to figure out what he was waiting for. A loud click echoed through the building, and then the sound of mechanical shutters clunked through. He opened the emergency exit, setting off the fire alarm again.

Lisa opened her mouth to speak, but then the world around her started to swirl and collapse, taking her breath away as it pulled her into darkness.

Alika took them to a safe house outside of town, out in the country where no one would think to look for a vampire. She ripped away from him the moment they arrived and looked around. Her eyes darted around before they finally settled on him. "Who are you?"

"My name is Alika." He looked at her. "I'm sure you want a shower and a good meal."

She licked her lips at the mention of a meal, but then she hesitated. "I have to feed from Romulus."

The name hit him hard, and he snarled. "Feed from him? Why?" He tried to think of any reason she'd need to feed from just one specific person.

She flinched back at his outrage. The fear in her eyes made his heart ache, and he took a deep breath. "Can you explain to me why it has to be him."

"I was told he was the only one who could satisfy the bloodlust. Occasionally, they let me feed from others, but it barely helps." She closed her eyes and wrapped her arms around her stomach.

He guided her to the couch and sat her down. The small room held only the couch and a chair, no television set, no table, nothing but places to sit. He settled her on the black fabric and touched her cheek. "When was the last time you ate?"

"I don't know," she whispered. "I'm so hungry, and I'm seeing things."

She was falling into the bloodlust. He cursed. "What's your name?"

"Lisa Thorne."

Okay, she at least remembered who she was, that was a good sign. "And how long have you been a vampire?"

"I don't know." She opened her eyes and looked at him. "I was out for my birthday, and my friends and I went to a supposedly haunted house." She gave a small laugh. "I…" She shook her head. "Never mind."

He wanted to know how the rest of the story went, but he needed just the basics right now. "When was that? Is that when you were changed?"

"I was turning thirty, January second, twenty-seventeen."

"Okay, so you've been a vampire less than a year. That's good to know." He stood and looked back at her. She looked a bit cleaner than when he saw her at the shipping yard. This close up, he could see the defined shape of her body under the shirt and jeans she now wore. "I'm going to get you to Zeek, and he'll figure out what to do with you." He stepped away from the couch toward the kitchen to make a call.

"Will he take me to be fed?"

He sighed. "I'll arrange for someone to come feed you. I have to find a paranormal creature and not a human."

"I told you only Romulus can take the bloodlust away; anyone else will only take the edge off."

"Who told you that?"

"Tara and Romulus."

"You can't trust them," he muttered. "Look, you stay here, I'm going to go chat with Zeek and then find a volunteer to feed you."

He watched her pull her knees up, and he knew he needed to find someone soon or she could end up on a killing spree trying to feed enough to sedate the bloodlust.

"I need to see Remus," she muttered.

He turned to tell her absolutely not but noticed she wasn't looking at him.

"I have a message for him. No, I can't just appear and disappear. I haven't learned. I've only done it a couple times by accident or luck."

Oh no, she was seeing things and talking to them. He'd suffered from the illusions of bloodlust before, but he didn't think any of them were friendly looking enough to chat up.

"What do you mean you need to see Remus?" he asked, pulling her attention away from whatever she was seeing.

She glanced at him and then away. "I need to get him a message. It's important that I see him as soon as I can. Please."

There was a small begging in her voice that pulled at his heart. He didn't give her an answer because it wasn't up to him. He'd mention it to Zeek and let the leader of vampires deal with it.

He went to the kitchen and dialed Zeek's number.

Lisa looked at the ghost that was sitting on the edge of the couch. She had no idea where she was or why he had brought her here. All she wanted to do was feed enough to take the edge off. She looked up when Alika left the room.

"I don't think he likes me much."

The woman laughed. "Alika doesn't like anyone. Don't take it personally. He just doesn't understand how to care for people. Give him time."

"How do you know him?" She didn't look back at the woman but kept her eyes on the kitchen doorway.

"I've seen him bring other Syndicate members here to talk. Or people who have information but need protection. I was one of those people."

Fear filled Lisa. "But you're dead."

"Not by his hand. I promise you."

Lisa nodded and was about to say something when Alika's voice caught her attention.

"Bad shape, Zeek. I need a wolf or something to feed her." There was a pause. "No, no idea when the last time she ate was. I'm not sure if we should have followed Casandra's advice on getting her. She keeps insisting that she needs to feed from Romulus. She muttered something about seeing Remus. I don't think she'll be able to tell the difference."

Lisa held her head down, what was he talking about 'tell the difference'? All she wanted to do was feed from Romulus so she could get out of the blood-lust.

Silence, but the ghost she had been talking to moved next to the kitch-en door as if trying to listen to more. Lisa pulled herself up off the couch and followed her.

"I don't think that's smart, Zeek, but if that's what you want to do. Yeah. Send one of the wolves over; I'll get her fed and then we'll figure things out. Have Skye search missing persons for a Lisa Thorne. I'll send a picture over for reference."

She peeked around the door jamb and watched him. The way he held himself reminded her of a wounded animal. Shoulders rounded just slightly to distract from his height and his body always tense.

He turned around and met her gaze. "Yeah, thanks." He hung the phone up and stuck it back in his pocket. "Did you hear the other end of that conversa-tion?"

She shook her head. "No, just your end."

"That's because we have special devices to block other creatures from hearing." He motioned to the doorway. "Come on, let's get you to the basement. You're exhausted, and it's not long before dawn."

She followed him out of the kitchen and back through the living room. He opened a door at the far end, and the dark stairwell seemed to close in as the damp smell of the basement hit her nose. "I don't want to be just locked away in another basement." There was a little more panic to her voice than she had wanted.

Alika palmed the wall and light flooded the stairwell. Cream-colored walls were almost too bright for her senses, but they were a welcome change to the black walls of her isolation chamber. "It's not as small as it looks. It's nothing like where you just came from. I'll be staying for the day as well."

She looked back at the ghost in the living room, and the ghost nodded. "Don't worry hon; it's nice down there. And he's right; he won't be leaving. Mostly to make sure you stay put."

Lisa rolled her eyes. "I already told you, I can't go anywhere."

"Who are you talking to? What kind of illusions are you having?" Alika put a hand on her shoulder. "Most vampires see horrible things in bloodlust."

"I see shadows, but I see other things when I'm not in bloodlust." She met his gaze, but she didn't expand on her thoughts. That's what got her in trouble with the agency. They figured out that she was different and locked her away.

Alika nodded slightly. "Uh huh. Okay, come on. Sun will be peaking over the horizon soon. Down we go."

She stepped past him and started down the stairs. The air around her grew colder with each step until she reached the bottom and saw a massive room with an oversized bed and a television mounted on the wall. Further was a door that was cracked open, and she saw a big tub inside. She relaxed almost instantly. "This is amazing."

"Nothing like where you came from. I'm sure you want to wash up, but I want you to rest before the wolf gets here. Once you're fed and I know you're not going to be seeing things and you're less likely to freak out, then you can take a bath and relax a little bit more."

"I don't sleep much," she admitted. "I'm sure that doesn't help with everything."

He gave her a gentle shove toward the bed. "Trust me, once you get in that bed, you'll sleep just fine."

"Before I was changed, I always thought vampires died at night." She crawled into the bed. The soft mattress engulfed her body, and she let out a deep sigh. She had no idea when the last time she felt a bed was, but this was heaven.

Alika chuckled. "No, we just weaken. If we died, then you would have gotten some rest while you were in that hellhole. Now close your eyes."

She listened to him and let her eyes shut. Soon she'd be able to feed enough to take the edge off and then she could find someone to take her to Romulus so she could truly feed. At the thought of Romulus, voices started to whisper around her again.

"Remus. Seek out Remus." It sounded like it was right next to her.

She rolled over, pulling the blanket on the bed around her as the voices continued. "After rest," she promised. "After food."

They seemed to drift further away, and she forced herself to relax into something that felt like sleep.

Alika watched her mutter in her sleep. She'd mentioned something interesting, that she saw other things. He wanted to push, but soon she wouldn't be his problem. Cassy had mentioned that Lisa was a medium, but he didn't really believe it. He'd get her settled, take her to Remus, and let him decide what to do with her.

Zeek had mentioned that all of this could be a ploy, and Alika had agreed. It was too strange that she was a new vampire who needed to be taught and claimed that she needed to get a message to Remus. But, as he watched her, Alika realized that she wasn't acting. The fear in her eyes was very real when he opened the door to the basement.

Her body shook with weakness from not feeding. He'd seen the way she moved at the docks, and there was no way that the Agency could have put on an act there for him.

She rolled over with a groan, and he tucked the blanket around her. He caught himself mid-gesture and clenched his fist. He couldn't get attached to her. He needed to let her be and move on.

She muttered to herself again, and she rolled halfway into a ball. Hunger pains, he saw the sweat bead on her forehead, damping her hair. He needed that wolf to get here, now.

He stayed by her side while she slept. He'd turned on some news for his own amusement to see what was going on. There was a brief recap of how the Agency was trying to cover up a mess where they had been accused of corruption. He snorted as Romulus appeared on the screen, just a recap of the original press conference.

The moment he spoke, Lisa's eye shot open and locked on to the television.

"Lisa?" Alika asked and put a hand on her arm. "Lisa, you okay?"

She turned red-tinted eyes to him, and he knew exactly what was going on. She was too far into bloodlust to control herself. She licked her lips and tilted her head. He heard what she did, the front door unlocking and opening. The wolf was here now. A wicked smile curved her face, and she shot past him and up the stairs. He followed her and grabbed her right before she launched herself at the wolf and into the sunlight.

The wolf jumped backward. "Woah there, chicky, we should at least exchange names."

"Really, not the time for manors William." Alika held Lisa by her shoulders, keeping her back from the rays of sunlight in the living room. The woman thrashed against him, throwing her body weight at the wolf, her fangs bared.

William walked in and shut the door behind him. "Okay yeah, I see that. She's not going to kill me is she?"

Alika shook his head. "I won't let her, but I can't promise she's going to be gentle." He picked Lisa up around the waist, pinning her arms to her side and carried her back down the stairs as she jerked around in his hold.

"That's okay; I like it rough on occasion." He laughed a little as he followed them down the stairs. Once they were all the way down, William held his hand out to Lisa. "Come on; clearly you need to feed." Alika let Lisa go. She lunged at William, taking him to the ground.

Alika flinched at the thud as the two of them hit the floor. Lisa snarled as she torn into the neck of the poor wolf, but Alika had to hand it to him, William simply stroked Lisa's hair and whispered to her as she fed from him.

The sharp smell of blood hit the air and Alika shuddered. He would need to feed when nightfall hit, but for now, he needed to make sure Lisa was taken care of and under control so they could visit Remus. He had no idea how the new vampire was going to react since it seemed she had some type of attachment to Romulus.

Of course, feeding from someone did create a metaphysical bonding. He tapped Lisa on the back after a few minutes. She looked back at him, blood dribbling down her chin. The red tint was gone from her eyes, but he saw something else there. Shame.

She wiped her mouth off with the back of her hand. "I'm sorry, I was just so hungry."

William sat up from the ground, a goofy grin on his face and his eyes half-hooded. "All good, no harm done."

"Nothing a little rest for William won't cure," Alika promised. "And now that you're fed, it's time to get us back to bed."

She nodded and stood, her movements were a little less shaky now, and he found himself relaxing a little bit. Her biggest need was taken care of, and now they could focus on the real problem. Who she was and why she really wanted to see Remus.

William got off the floor and wandered toward the stairs. "You two have a good day; I'm just going to park myself on the couch upstairs. I'll be around at dusk so you can feed again."

"I'll be fine for a while." She shook her head and walked back towards the bed. "It's always a long time between feedings; I'm used to it." She rubbed her arms as if she was cold and Alika suppressed a growl; something was making her nervous.

William paused at the bottom step. "Dude, she doesn't know what she's doing. Even out of control she should know how to feed properly."

"I don't think her maker taught her." Alika watched her snuggle into the blanket. "I think there's something going on here and it's not what Zeek and I thought."

William waved a hand. "Don't worry about me. You go take care of the baby vampire."

"Thanks, man, rest up." Alika watched William climb the stairs and then turned to the bed only to find Lisa curled up already fast asleep.

He studied the way her hair fell over her face, and it reminded him a lot of his wife. He put a hand to his heart; there was something about this woman that triggered memories of his family.

Alika sat down and moved Lisa's hair out of her face. She still breathed as if she were alive, but her skin was cold and pale. "So what happened to you, Lisa Thorne?"

"Kidnapped," she whispered and curled up. "Taken."

He frowned and thought about what she'd told him earlier. He assumed that she was an employee of the Agency and maybe she wasn't supposed to be changed. He hadn't thought she was actually kidnapped.

His phone buzzed, and he found a file sent to him via text from Skye. He clicked on it, and a missing person report came up for Lisa Thorne. It was her alright. Not as sickly looking, but the same dark hair and hazel eyes. She was smiling in the picture, which was something she had yet to do for him. He'd only seen the terrifying smirk that crossed her face when she was in bloodlust. She'd been missing for five months according to the report.

As a new vampire, she would need to feed every night, but it sounded like the agency was starving her for some reason. Maybe to get information out of her, maybe she had a connection that he didn't know about. A secret Syndicate spy caught by the agency?

He growled, and her eyes fluttered open. "I'm sorry, I didn't mean to wake you. You should sleep."

"I don't sleep much." She sat up and pulled the blanket up to her chest. "Between the nightmares and the voices, there's no way to sleep peacefully."

Voices? "Are you psychic?"

"That's what Romulus thinks I am." She looked away from him. "Or at least that's what he tells Tara."

"Who is Tara?" He tried not to sound frustrated, but she was speaking about the situation as if he was supposed to know every detail.

She sighed. "My handler, the woman who's in charge of me."

She had a keeper, and the woman hadn't done a very good job with her. "She tortured you."

"No, there was no real torture involved. She punished me if I did something wrong. But if I gave them the answers they wanted, then I was returned to my cell."

"How many times have you fed since you were there?" he demanded. "Starving is torture."

She flinched at his voice, and he sighed. "I'm sorry, I've been there. That's the only reason I know. Starving is a form of torture for vampires. Controlling when and who they feed from, torture. You can't tell me that you didn't feel pain when you were hungry."

Lisa hung her head. "Four times."

"In five months." Horror filled him. "It's amazing that you had any strength at all." He pulled her to him and held her; to his surprise, she curled against him.

After a few minutes of silence, he broke away from her. "Your family has been looking for you. They put in a missing person report."

"I don't think they'll want to see me like this," she muttered. "My parents are like me, and they've seen the deaths caused by vampires."

He jerked at that. "Not all vampires are murderers. Is that what you think?"

"No, but that's how they do." She shook her head. "It's better that they think I'm dead."

Family had been everything to him at one point, to see her give up on hers broke his heart.

She scooted off the bed. "I'm going to go soak in the bath now."

"Of course." He laid back. "I'm going to take a quick nap while you do that."

She didn't look back at him as she disappeared into the bathroom.

Lisa started the bath, turning the water as hot as the handle would allow. She stripped her clothes off and looked at herself in the mirror. Where was the woman who'd been so confident? So strong?

Gone.

She closed her eyes and sighed. No, this couldn't be the end of her. She could feel her body warming from the blood she drank earlier. She'd just changed. She could adapt to this. This was just a different life. A new life. A life where she had no one to turn to. When Alika first rescued her, he'd told her to go back from where she came from. She wasn't welcome here, and she couldn't go home. Her family was clear about vampires; they were the worst of all the supernatural creatures out there. They wouldn't want her, and that broke her heart, her spirit. She choked on the sob that tried to bubble up. She'd never see her sister again, and they'd been thick as thieves. No more late nights watching television, no more family dinners, no more walking around the fields together.

Alone. She was alone now.

Turning, she looked at the bath and sighed. "One day at a time."

"That's right, one day at a time." The female ghost from before was sitting on the edge of the tub. "You're fed, rested, and now you can assess everything."

Lisa slipped into the bath. "I don't want to assess everything. I want someone to teach me how this crap is supposed to work."

"Then ask Alika to."

The hot water slipped around her skin, coaxing her muscles to relax. "I don't think he wants to teach me."

"I told you, he's just rough on the outside. He tried to nurse me back to health; he tried to take care of me. Don't let him fool you. He has a soft spot for people in need."

Lisa closed her eyes and dunked her head under the water. "And what happened to you? I haven't seen your death."

"Mmm, the death was uneventful. I died in my sleep on a couch upstairs. However, that couch has since been removed, so it looks really funny, I'm basically in the middle of the couch." She chuckled. "You'll see it I'm sure. I died right before midnight."

"Who killed you?" Lisa splashed the water over her arms, and she rubbed it over the skin. Normally feeding made her feel dirty, but this time there wasn't the sense of filth on her.

"Agency. Poison shut down my body. I was in withdrawals so bad that I started having seizures and there just wasn't anything Alika could do."

"I don't know anything about the Agency other than what I've seen with Tara and what I heard before I was taken. I thought they were the good guys."

"That's a facade for the public," Alika's voice came from the door.

Lisa squealed and sank down further into the tub. "What are you doing in here?"

"I heard you talking, and I wanted to see who you were talking to. But I think I know what you meant by voices now."

She looked away from him, not wanting to admit it. "I don't know what you're talking about. Already told you Romulus thinks I'm psychic."

"But that's not what you are. You're a medium. I didn't believe Cassy when she told me." He leaned against the door jamb. "And I bet being a vampire did something to any of the control you had. Am I right?"

She stared at the water. "The night I was changed it was like a veil lifted up, and suddenly instead of just getting feelings and seeing outlines, they were screaming at me and clear as day. Like I've gone crazy."

"What did Romulus want with you? Why did he make sure to keep you weak and dependent?"

She shook her head. "I don't want to talk about it. What I need to do is see Remus, give him a message, and then I'll be out of your hair." Not that she had any place to go. The thought hit her hard again, and she sniffled as tears started to form in her eyes.

"Aw, come on Lisa, don't start crying. I'll get you to Remus tonight, and then we'll figure out what to do with you from there."

"You didn't want me before, what's changed?"

He shook his head. "I didn't want to be the one to take care of you, and that's my own issue and not one for you to worry about. Okay?"

"Yes, sir," she muttered and traced her fingers over the water. "There's a ghost here; she says you cared for her, that you did what you could for her."

"Oh, don't drag me into this." The ghost shook her head. "He doesn't want to remember me."

Alika nodded. "Overdose victim of the new drug the Agency is pushing out. She wasn't able to survive the withdrawals; it was harsh. Luckily she died peacefully. But you're right, I did everything I could, and she still died. Like people before her did. This is why I don't want you in my care."

He turned to leave, and she studied his backside, his black shirt clung to his body, hanging over the jeans that hugged his ass. She smiled a little bit. It'd been a long time since she could admire a man's body.

"Stop staring." The ghost laughed. "I know he's got a nice ass, but you need to get cleaned up and figure out where you're going after Remus."

Maybe she'd get lucky and Remus would have an idea of where she could go, maybe there was like a vampire sanctuary. She laughed at the thought, and Alika turned around and faced her again. "The ghost say something funny?"

"No, I just had a thought, and it made me chuckle." She smiled at him. "Thank you."

"For what?"

"Not calling me crazy."

He nodded. "We all have our interesting quirks. Yours just happens to be that you can talk to ghosts. I'll let you and Krystal talk. Enjoy your bath."

He walked out and shut the door behind him, and she smiled as she leaned her head against the tub.

"You're happy," Krystal said. "Because he didn't call you crazy?"

"When you go through life being able to hear and see things you aren't supposed to, a lot of people call you crazy. It's refreshing."

"Good, because you're not really crazy." Krystal faded into the air. "I'll give you some time to relax."

Lisa closed her eyes and took a few deep breaths. She didn't need to breathe, she knew that, but it still helped her focus. The problem was, all she could focus on was Alika. How kind he'd been since they'd gotten to the house, how handsome he was, and how powerful he felt when he held her.

23

CHAPTER THREE

Alika watched Lisa sleep through the day. She might not have been lying when she said she didn't sleep much, but it didn't mean she wasn't exhausted. After her bath, she had crawled right into bed without even worrying about clothes or drying her hair.

He'd gotten William to get her clean clothing during the day so that she had something to wear that didn't have days of dirt caked into it.

She rolled up over and looked at him. "I'm sorry, I passed out."

"You were exhausted. Let's get you fed and then we'll take you to Remus to deliver your message."

She tilted her head to the side. "I'm fine; I don't need to feed again until the bloodlust comes back. It'll be a couple days."

"No, you need to feed once a night; it'll help you with your control and show you that it's not just Romulus' blood that can sedate the bloodlust."

She looked away, and he sighed. "I'm sorry, I don't mean to make you feel ashamed of what the Agency has forced you to do. I just want to help you so that you can live a normal life."

"So that you don't have to take care of me," she corrected. "That's fine. I'll leave once I talk to Remus. I want nothing to do with this mess anyway."

He didn't miss the tone of her voice. "You shouldn't be in this mess. This is a fight for the ages, Syndicate vs. Agency. Romulus shouldn't have dragged you into it."

24

"He didn't. Someone else changed me and left me for dead." She sat up and pulled the blanket up to her chest. "I stumbled into the Agency building because I thought they were supposed to help. Instead, Tara took me to Romulus."

She started shaking and shook her head. "I hadn't fed yet. All I wanted was help. I thought they were going to help me."

That bastard. He wrapped his fingers around hers and squeezed. "What happened?"

"He fed me, and it was the most delicious thing I'd ever tasted. I wanted more, but he refused." She looked at him. "He exchanged information for food. Whatever I could tell him. Once he could verify it somehow, then he'd have Tara take me to him to feed."

Alika cupped her cheek in his hand. "That is not normal, that's not how things are supposed to work. There are people who volunteer to feed you."

"Like William?"

"Like William, and he's waiting for you upstairs." He smiled and dropped his hand. "There are clean clothes for you on the foot of the bed." There was just one thing he couldn't figure out. "Lisa, how did Romulus figure out what you were?"

She sighed. "I was screaming about the voices. They're so overwhelming now that I can't block them out, I couldn't do anything but listen to them scream at me. There were a bunch at the Agency."

"So he put it together and decided to use you." He shook his head. "Don't worry, that's not the way Remus works."

"I just want to get this under control and find a new life."

He wanted to be part of that life, though he didn't know how. "A new life? Not your old life?"

She shook her head. "No, I told you, I can't go back to that."

He didn't miss the sorrow in her voice. "What if I talked to your family?"

"You'd do that for me? I've already told you they think all vampires are evil."

He shrugged. "Because I know that when my life fell to pieces that all I wanted was for it to go back to normal. If I could give that to you, I would." He stood. "Go on and get dressed. I'll be upstairs with William."

He walked up the steps and closed the basement door, leaning against it. Could he deliver her back to her family and walk out of her life? He didn't know, but it was something that needed to be done. She wanted a normal life; she should have it and not have to worry about the Syndicate and the Agency.

He looked at William and held a hand up. "Not a word, wolf."

The man chuckled. "Aw come on, you look like someone kicked your puppy."

"Not true. I need to make a phone call before she gets up here." He shook his head and started to the front door. "It's not something I want you hearing either."

William held his hands up. "As you wish, oh grumpy bloodsucker. You want me to feed her when she gets up here?"

"Yes, she should be more gentle this time." So he hoped. Of course, no one had taught her how to bite. He rubbed his eyes. "Okay no, wait until I get back and I'll help her with her latch, so she doesn't tear another chunk out of you."

"Sounds like a plan."

Alika stepped out of the house. He walked down the dirt road a few yards to make sure he wouldn't be overheard. He didn't want Lisa or the wolf to hear even his end of the conversation.

He dialed the number Skye had sent along with the missing person's report and let it ring through.

"Hello?" a soft female voice answered. "This is the Thorne residence."

"Hello, Ms. Thorne? My name is Alika, and I've located your daughter."

Lisa came up the stairs after getting dressed in the clean jeans and t-shirt William managed to get her. "Where's Alika?"

"He had a phone call to make, so he stepped outside for a bit. We're supposed to wait for him to get back to feed you. So you don't take another chunk out of me."

His voice was joking, but she still felt bad. "I'm sorry, I was just so hungry."

"Hey, it's okay. We never got properly introduced. I'm William, and you are?" He held his hand out to her, a lopsided smile on his face.

She shook his hand. "I'm Lisa Thorne."

"It's nice to meet you, Lisa. Welcome back to the world." He leaned back on the couch. "It's not much, but I'm sure it beats being in the Agency's care."

"Alika tell you where I was?"

"All he said was that the Agency had you and neglected to teach you the most basic things about being a vampire. I've been there before; they aren't nice people."

So she knew. "I'm sorry you had to experience that."

"Don't be; I'd do it again if I had to. I was protecting members of my pack." His eyes went distant a little bit, and then he shook his head. "That's neither here nor there though."

She wanted to ask, but knowing her own reservations about explaining her experience, she didn't feel it was appropriate. "Well, hopefully, I can find someone to teach me, and I can move forward." She tilted her head as she heard footsteps approaching the house. "Alika's back."

"So he is." William looked towards the door, and a moment later it opened. "You ready to teach the baby vampire?"

Lisa licked her lips at the thought of more blood. It wasn't Romulus' for sure, but it still helped push the hunger away.

Alika nodded. "Okay, Lisa, you don't have to tear into him. Take his wrist."

William held his wrist out, and she wrapped her fingers around his arm. She could feel his pulse vibrate against her skin and she felt the need to feed fill her again.

"Control yourself." Alika put a hand on her shoulder. "Think about what you're doing. Use your fangs to bite down and then drink from the puncture marks."

She nodded and wrapped her lips around William's wrist, she bit down and let the blood drip into her mouth. The copper tasting liquid hit her tongue, and she tried not to moan as she sucked on the wound, drawing more of the substance into her mouth.

This is what feeding without a frenzy felt like. Wonderful, just a good meal to fill her stomach. She pulled back and licked a drop of blood off her lips.

"Good job. See how much more control you have when you feed closer together?" Alika smiled at her. "Now, let's go. I've arranged a meeting with Remus."

She closed her eyes and took a moment to enjoy feeling full. "Okay." She opened her eyes and kissed William's cheek. "Thank you."

"Anytime, if you need me, just give me a call. I'm happy to help."

She stood from the couch and looked at Alika. "How long will it take us to drive?"

He shook his head. "We're not driving; we're going to use an ability that vampires have. You've used it before, at the shipping yard."

She stared at him. "The shipping yard? You were there?"

"Yeah, I was there checking something out for the Syndicate. That's when I first saw you."

She thought she had sensed another vampire, but then again, she was too busy with all the voices around her. "Why didn't you get me then?"

"Because I couldn't fight against massive amounts of Agency people with guns. It was just an observation mission because of the increased activity at the docks. The Agency tried to take over one of our docks, and we wanted to know exactly what was going on."

"They are shipping humans out," she spat out without thinking.

He nodded. "I know, we weren't sure how many or where they were getting them. I was hoping to get more information than that."

"So you just stood there and let them make plans to ship them out?" Her voice raised a pitch. "Can't we go to the police or something?"

He shook his head. "I'm going to get Remus the information about what I found, and he'll work on a plan. The police are useless in this situation because the Agency has people in the police. We can't risk them learning what we know."

Anger welled up in her. "So they are just getting away with this shit?"

"It's an ongoing battle Lisa, and you can help us by giving Remus his message and answering any questions that he might have."

Which meant that Remus could use her too, but maybe the Syndicate was the right side of the battle to be on. "I don't know if I can answer his questions."

"That's fine, all you have to do is try." He put a hand on her shoulder. "Are you ready to face the leader of the Syndicate?"

She swallowed. "As ready as I'll ever be, I guess."

"That'a girl."

The world around them swirled and disappeared into darkness.

Alika opened his eyes as they appeared in the office building that the Syndicate used for most of their basic meetings. Lisa swayed a little bit next to him, and he put an arm around her to help steady her. The way she fit against his side perfectly made him sigh. He could hold her forever, but she wasn't his, and they had a meeting to get to.

She looked around and suddenly threw her hands over her ears. "Make them stop. Make them stop," she cried, and he cupped her face with his hands.

"Lisa?"

"So many voices. So many dead." She gasped and ripped away from him. She ran for the front door, nearly tripping over her own feet, and he quickly flashed in front of her to stop her.

"Lisa, Remus is waiting for us upstairs. I need you to focus, block them out."

She looked up at him with wide eyes. "I can't. I don't know how. They're all screaming at me."

He grabbed his phone from his and his earbuds from his pocket. He scrolled through to find the loudest music he could and caught her attention. "Try this."

She gave him a confused look but did as told, putting the earbuds in. He could see the tension leaving her body as she relaxed to the music. He smiled and held his hand out to her to guide her to the upper floor.

Her fingers tangled with his and she squeezed them as if saying thank you. She didn't pull back, and he didn't want to let her hand go, so they walked together through the empty lobby to the elevators. The business building was just a front, the lobby was always abandoned, there was no receptionist, and the first couple floors were for Syndicate use for things like security and records. The basement held the server room and interrogation rooms, which he was sure were the cause of Lisa's problems right now.

They were silent as they rode up in the elevator. He noted how adorable she looked when her face wasn't scrunched up in horror. Her hair was tucked behind one ear, while the other side fell over her shoulder, and her eyes searched the elevator, drinking in every detail. Her gaze landed on him, and she smiled, showing her dainty little fangs...which made his cock stir. They couldn't feed from each other for nourishment, but he wanted to feel her fangs buried into his neck while he took her against the elevator wall.

He turned away. He needed to control himself, and that elevator couldn't move fast enough for his liking.

The doors finally dinged and opened. He led Lisa out, and she still looked around, her eyes a bit wide as they walked down the carpeted hall that led to the office Remus used. Normally this was reserved for Syndicate leaders, but Zeek was letting him handle this one.

The office door was cracked open, and Alika walked in with Lisa by his side.

The leader of the Syndicate sat at the head of the table, his button-down shirt opened a few buttons, his tie was loose around his neck, and his silver hair was pulled away from his face, but what set Remus apart from most creatures roaming the world was his swirling eyes.

Lisa stiffened next to him and let out a small whimper. She reached up and pulled the earbuds out. "Romulus. You brought me back to Romulus."

He could hear the panic in her voice as her eyes searched the room and she stepped back. "I thought you weren't going to take me back to them. I...I trusted you."

Remus stood. "You have me mistaken for my brother."

She froze, and Alika reached out for her hand to stop her from bolting for the door. He followed her gaze, and it wasn't focused on Remus, it was focused just behind him.

"You promise he won't harm me?" she whispered. Remus started to answer, but Alika held his hand up.

"She's not talking to you or me. Give her a second."

Remus glared at him and crossed his arms. "I have another meeting tonight. Deliver your message."

Lisa nodded and looked at Remus. "You're a demi-god, which explains so much about Romulus and you."

Remus jerked a little bit. "And who told you that, little vampire?"

"Your mother."

In an instant, Remus had Lisa pinned to the wall by her shoulders. Alika put a hand on his shoulder. "Back up. She's new; she doesn't know her strength or yours. Stop scaring her."

Remus shrugged him off. "My mother has been dead for centuries."

"I know." Lisa remained calm. "She's not forgotten you, she's always with you, approving of your leadership, your goals, your bloodline."

Remus stepped back, allowing Lisa a bit of room. "My bloodline?"

She stared at the woman, the same silver hair that Remus had flowed down her back, and she wore a classic Roman dress that moved around her. Lisa couldn't peel her eyes away from the beautiful woman behind Remus, despite the demigod being so close to her. "You have blood relatives in this world. There's one that the Agency has gotten a hold of, and you need to make sure she's rescued. Her name is Malia, and they're holding her at the docks." Lisa tried not to stumble over her words, repeating exactly what the ghost had told her to.

"Very good," the ghost whispered, "now tell him the rest of your story."

The ghost had managed to fill in some of the gaps, but Lisa needed to explain how she came to this knowledge. "I was taken to the docks after Tara took me to examine an old drug warehouse. The ghosts there, they screamed about Malia and told me that I had to get to you and tell you she was there."

She watched Remus' face for any signs of anger or violence, but he turned away from her.

"Thank you; I will deal with it. Alika, make sure Lisa is taken care of. Help her know how to be a vampire and not kill in my area, or she'll draw the attention of the Agency. I doubt she wants to go back there."

Lisa cringed. "I don't, but I don't want to stay with the Syndicate either."

"I never said you were staying. I haven't decided if you'd be a big enough asset to keep. I said Alika would make sure you know how to behave properly; then we'll discuss where you're going."

She tried to wrap her mind around his phrasing. It seemed odd, not quite a threat, but not really a friendly response either. "Thank you." She spun around to leave but hesitated at the door. Would the voices start screaming at her if she left the room?

"Earbuds," Alika whispered and put a hand on the small of her back. "They seemed to help last time."

She nodded, put them in again, and hit play on the phone. Alika led her back to the elevator, silent as they walked and rode it down. The voices simply became background noise against the loud music in her ears. For the first time since she had been turned, she couldn't really hear them, and she didn't have to fight against them.

Alika tapped her arm. "Can you hear me?"

"I can, just enough." Maybe it was the vampire hearing; maybe it was because he wasn't a ghost and it was more of a direct noise.

"Good, I think we need to stop and get you an mp3 player and some headphones."

She hung her head. "I don't think I've got any money in my account, never mind the card to my account."

"Don't worry, my gift." He squeezed her hand just as the elevator door opened. They walked out, and he smiled down at her. "We have one more stop for the night."

There was a sense of hesitation in his voice; it'd dropped down from the happy tone he'd used talking about the mp3 player. "Where?"

He pressed his lips together. "I contacted your family."

Her heart fell. "What? No. I told you they wouldn't want to see me."

"But you also told me you wanted to go back to a normal life." He sighed. "They were happy to hear from me. I've already told them about your change."

She cringed. "What did they say?" She tried not to get her hopes up. Would they accept her now? She remembered all the sermons they'd heard at church, all the talks about how vampires were against God's creations and his will. How they were of the Devil himself.

"They want to see you. They understand that you didn't choose this life, that someone forced it." He hugged her and put his head on top of hers. "They want you home."

She threw her arms around him. "Thank you. Oh my God, thank you." She pulled away and wiped the tears coming from her eyes.

He wiped the red-tinged liquid from her hand. "Let's go then?"

She took a deep breath to calm herself. "Yeah, let's go. I can't thank you enough." She closed her eyes as the world around her disappeared.

Her body hummed as they reappeared somewhere. She looked around the familiar yet strange fields. The hot and humid air hit her body as the wind danced over the ground, bringing the smell and taste of smoke to her nose.

Panic forced her feet forward, one moment she was standing next to Alika and next she found herself in front of what should have been a one-story farmhouse. Except it was wood pillars covered in flames now.

Alika appeared by her side, and he pulled her away. "Come on; it's not safe."

"What happened?" She couldn't take her eyes off the flames. She pulled her arm away from him and took a step closer. The wood cracked and fell, destroying what was left of the roof frame and sending embers dancing around. She could see the outline of bodies through the smoke, and she put a hand to her mouth as a sob escaped.

"We need to go, Lisa." His voice raised a pitch, and he wrapped his fingers around her wrist right as the sound of a gunshot echoed through the area.

The world around her melted away, and when it reappeared they were in the living room of the safe house, and blood covered Alika's stomach.

CHAPTER FOUR

Lisa looked at him, and her mind froze on what she was supposed to do. She had never had to treat a gunshot wound; she didn't even know what to do to treat a vampire. "Krystal!" she called, hoping the ghost would know what to do.

"Don't call her; she's dealt with enough bloodshed." Alika hissed as he pressed his hand to the stomach. "There's a first aid kit in the kitchen, go get it." He laid back on the couch. Even for a vampire, he was looking pretty pale.

She ran to the kitchen and flung open cupboards trying to find the white box. When she finally found it, she snatched it up and went back to the living room. Alika's eyes were closed, and his hand against his stomach was limp.

"Oh, God, Alika?" her voice squeaked as she ran to him and started looking for a pulse. He didn't have a pulse. "No, no no."

His eyes popped open. "I'm a vampire; we don't have pulses."

She snorted and choked on a half sob. "You scared me."

"You're going to have to pull the bullet out. It's silver, and it's keeping me from healing."

She looked at all the blood and then to him. "What?"

"Find the tweezers and dig the bullet out. Get some gloves if you're squeamish, but get it the fuck out of me."

She dug in the white box and grabbed the tweezers. She took a deep breath and looked at the wound. Blood oozed out of it. She needed to clean it first so she could see inside. She went to the bathroom and found a rag. She wet it and returned to the couch.

"You don't have to worry about me catching an infection. Once the bullet is out, I'll heal," he promised and grabbed her hand. "Clean it up, get it out. Got it?"

"Got it." She wiped the blood off and cussed as it continued to flow from the wound. He flinched, and something silver in the wound caught her attention. "I see it." She took a deep breath, and her shaking hand started toward the wound. He held her wrist.

"Steady, you've got this."

She slowly put the tips of the tweezers in and pinched the bullet. She pulled it out quickly and put it on the table.

He grabbed her hand and kissed it. "Good job. Now watch the magic."

She looked down and watched as the skin knitted itself back together leaving only a smear of blood. "That's amazing."

"A perk of being a vampire." He laughed and leaned up and kissed her.

She was stunned for a moment but kissed him back. "How come your blood doesn't drive me into a frenzy?"

"Because there's no substance to it." He pressed his forehead to hers.

There was a strange sense of comfort to him now. He was her only hope of navigating this crazy new world. She closed her eyes at the thought. This was her new world.

Alika wrapped his arms around her. "I'm sorry about your family."

Her heart shattered at the sudden reminder. Everything she ever had was gone. She'd pushed it away in the moment of panic at having to pull a bullet out of him. She lifted her head and met his gaze. "They're gone."

"The Agency probably did it. We'll go back tomorrow and examine the destruction. I'll have some of our people secure the scene today."

"You mean kill the agents that are there," she corrected. "Just more violence, more death." She ran her hands over her eyes as she started to cry. "It's needless killing. My family is dead because of some stupid turf war." She shoved him away and tried to stand up.

He wrapped his arms around her again and held her tight. "So is mine."

That jerked her back to reality. "What?"

"Back when Romulus and Remus were both fighting to control Rome, before Remus was thought to be dead. Romulus sent troops to my village. I barely made it in time to help fight the troops off. It was too late for my family. He'd slaughtered my wife and my children because he knew that the village supported Remus. I almost died in the battle; I was changed to save my life." The ever-present shadows behind him started to make sense, his family.

She sank into him. "But why does the Syndicate kill so many people. I heard the ghosts in that building. They were tortured."

"War isn't pretty, Lisa, we do what we have to in order to get information on the Agency, sometimes that includes torturing people."

She felt herself shrink away. From a quiet country life, thrown into the chaotic world of paranormal creatures. "Have you tortured people?"

"No, but I've killed. I'd kill without hesitation to protect people I love and those who can't defend themselves." He nodded. "Like you. I'd kill for you."

She should have been flattered. "You wanted me to just go back to where I came from." She shook her head. "Something has changed your mind."

"You had a family, a life; I thought that you had just simply been in the wrong place at the wrong time. But now the agency seems to have planned this. They are purposely taking everything away from you...and it's all too familiar to me." He ran a hand through his hair and then stood, leaving her on the floor. "You need to clean up, so do I. Go ahead and go downstairs; I'll shower up here."

He walked off without a glance back at her. She sat on the floor, confused as to what she did wrong. One moment he was comforting her, and then the next he seemed to be mad at the world. There was no winning with him, and now she was alone in her grief, which was the last thing she wanted.

Alika stripped his ruined shirt off and threw it in the bathroom trash. He wanted to offer Lisa comfort, but he was starting to get lost in his own grief. Her embrace chased away the cobwebs and made him feel again, but the death of her family, the burning of her house, it hadn't just been the Agency's way of trying to destroy her hope, it'd been a sign to him too.

Because it was exactly how his family had been killed.

He did not doubt that he would find the remains of Lisa's family in the sitting room, with evidence of their murder, throats cut to the point of near decapitation. He closed his eyes at the thought. Romulus was ruthless, and so were his agents.

He turned on the water and let the hot spray flow over his body. Lisa was going to end up needing family, a mentor, someone who could help her be a vampire, and it wasn't going to be him because she didn't like violence. Her ability would drive her crazy with all the voices on Syndicate properties. He'd have to find someone else who could teach her.

He knew that he needed to, but doing it was something completely different. He didn't want to let her go.

He washed and got out of the shower. After drying off, he transported himself down to the basement, leaving the towel in the bathroom upstairs.

He paused when he realized Lisa was sitting on the bed, a red towel wrapped around her body, the tip of it tucked between her ample breasts, threatening to fall with each breath she took. The need to do human things was still enduring; she hadn't been dead long enough to realize that she didn't have to breathe.

She had her eyes closed and had yet to acknowledge that he was in the room. He stalked towards her, crawling on to the bed and then moving behind her. She still didn't move, but her body tensed, frozen in her spot as he started to run his fingers through her hair.

"What are you doing?" There was a small hitch in her voice.

He pressed his lips to her neck. "I'm untangling your hair; it'll be a mess if it dries like this."

She turned to look at him. "I can brush it."

"Don't. Let me." He disappeared into the bathroom and grabbed a brush. He came back out, and she still sat right where he left her. Taking the brush, he slowly worked his way through her hair, starting at her tips and continuing up.

She let out a small sigh as he eased his way through the tangles, separating sections and slowly working through the thick locks. Bit by bit she started to relax. When he finished, he set the brush down on a nightstand.

He wrapped his arms around her and kissed her neck again. "Much better."

"Where did you learn how to be so gentle?" She turned and kissed his cheek. "As a warrior, I wouldn't have expected it."

He chuckled. "I had a wife; she taught me many things. How to be gentle was one of them." He ran his hands over her arms. "But I don't want to think about her right now. I want to think about you."

She let out a soft moan as he kissed her neck again. "I'm okay with that."

He slowly turned her around to face him. "Good." He cupped her face in his hands and pulled her lips to his. She wrapped her arms around him and pulled him closer.

Lisa crushed her lips to his and held him tight against her. The towel slipped out from between them, and she led him backward on the bed, their naked bodies brushing up against each other. This wasn't where she had expected the night to lead, but it was a welcomed distraction.

His hands slid down to her ass, cupping it tight enough that she could feel his nails dig into her skin. It only encouraged her. She pulled back and kissed down his jaw and over his neck, nipping every so slightly with her new fangs.

Alika let out a low, feral growl, and he flipped her over, so he was on top. He returned her little love nips with harder bites, his fangs pressed into her skin without breaking, but enough to draw out a moan from her. He traced his fingers down her body and in between her legs.

His finger found her slick folds and rubbed gently as his hot mouth danced crossed her skin, ending at her breasts. Her back arched up to him. His fangs scrapped over her nipple, causing her to gasp.

She rocked her hips into his hand, and he slipped a finger into her sex, moving it to the rhythm of her rocking. She grabbed his cock, wrapping her hand around it tightly. He threw his head back and moaned as her hand moved up and down his shaft.

He grabbed her wrist and pulled it away. She tilted her head to the side, questioning him until he thrust into her. She cried out at the sudden penetration. He slowly moved out of her, only to slam back in, this time the cry turned into a whimper of pleasure as her muscles tightened around him.

They moved together in a rhythm until she put a hand on his chest. He stopped and kissed her gently. "What?"

She gave him a wicked grin, looking at him from under her lashes in a coy manner. "I want to be on top."

He flipped them over without missing a beat. She spread her hands over his chiseled chest and slowly rocked her hips, drawing him in and out as she did. He put his hands on her hips guiding her as she moved faster.

She moaned and bowed her head. Her hair traced over his chest as they moved. The pleasure started to build in her, tightening her core around him. His fingers dug into her hips as she increased her speed.

The orgasm crashed into her, stealing the air from her lungs as the pleasure stormed through her body wave after wave. Alika held tight to her as his own orgasm came. Lisa curled up by his side as the pleasure faded from her. She laid her head on his chest, and he stroked her hair.

"Dawn's coming."

She nodded. "Yeah. I'm good here. I'll deal with everything come nightfall." It probably wasn't healthy, but for now, she could pretend that everything in her world was perfect, because that's how Alika made it feel.

Alika pulled the blanket over Lisa as she fell asleep. He laid there for a few minutes afterward, playing with her hair and imagining that this could be their new life. Except she didn't approve of the Syndicate and that was his job, recon missions, killing where needed, torture if it came to it. He closed his eyes; she'd come so far in the couple days he'd known her. She was strong, and with music blaring, she could probably ignore the voices around her.

"Krystal," he muttered, "If you're around, I really could use some help with this. She's the first woman I've wanted to stay with since my wife."

He felt something warm pass through him, and he wondered for a moment if it was Krystal trying to tell him something. "I don't want to see her die at the hand of the Agency, but I don't think Syndicate is where she belongs."

No physical response this time, and he sighed. He slipped out from under Lisa and waited for her to settle before he got off the bed. He needed to find a way to protect her. Maybe he could put her in some type of witness protection program. If the Agency knew where she was, then they would go after her again. So she'd need to know how to protect herself. How to hide.

He paced the room wondering what favors he could call in to keep her safe. There had to be someone. He rubbed his eyes and reached for his phone to call an old friend. He never thought he'd have to reach out to him like this.

He clicked on the name and waited for the phone to ring.

"General, what's up?" Tyson's voice came over the line. "It's been a while."

"I need someone I can trust that's not Syndicate or Agency." He looked over at Lisa, and his heart broke at the thought of sending her away, but it was what would be best.

Tyson hesitated. "I don't want to get wrapped up in this fight. I retired centuries ago; you know that."

"I know, but she's not either, and she doesn't belong in this war." Even he could hear the desperation in his voice.

"She?" Tyson sighed. "Who is she?"

Alika resisted the urge to call her his love or his mate. "She's a new vampire and a medium. She just needs a safe place to lay low and someone who can teach her."

"And what's her relation to you? It's not like you to go out of the way to protect someone like this. Not since…" he let the words trail off, and Alika knew exactly what he was talking about.

"Don't worry about what she is to me. She needs to be safe. Can you help me out?"

Tyson was silent for a moment. "I can't take her forever, but I can help her build a new life if that's what you want, Alika. Or more importantly, what she wants."

"Yeah, it's what she wants." But it wasn't what he wanted; he was having second thoughts. "I'll bring her to you tonight. Promise me you'll keep her safe?"

"What on earth is after her that you think I can't protect her?"

He rubbed his eyes. "She was an unwilling asset to the Agency."

"Great, we're going to have to leave the state, if not the country." Tyson sighed. "Seriously, they don't like to let their assets go."

He knew that, and that's why she had to get far away. "Start with leaving the state. The Agency killed her family, so we don't have to worry about her going back to them or contacting them."

"I'll see you tonight then, get her fed before you bring her here so I don't have to worry about it and we can travel the moment you arrive."

"Understood. Thank you, Tyson. I owe you one."

"You owe me a lot more than one, but who's keeping count." Tyson snorted and disconnected the call. Alika looked down at Lisa as she slept. She would be safer this way. She didn't know anything about this world.

He curled up next to her and pulled her close. Sleeping with her had been a stupid idea, but she called to him, her mind, soul, and body, he wanted it all, and he'd been so fucking stupid by giving in.

CHAPTER FIVE

Lisa woke up when she felt the sun sink below the horizon. It was a different feeling waking up in a soft bed than waking up from poor rest in her isolation chamber. What was even better was Alika's arms wrapped around her and his face buried in her neck.

She rolled over and sighed. This she could get used to, his arms made the world around her disappear. But she'd have to face reality, and she needed to face the death of her family. "Alika?"

"Hm?" He pulled her closer, nuzzling her neck.

"I want to go see the house with you."

His head shot up, and he met her gaze. "I don't think that's a good idea."

"I need some closure. Please." She sighed. "I just need to see that that part of my life is over."

He brushed her cheek with his hand. "If you want, it should be safe since the Syndicate secured it. I need to take you somewhere safe afterward."

"What do you mean?"

"I mean that I'm taking you away from the fight between the Agency and the Syndicate. You're going to be safe and get a chance to start your new life."

Her heart fell. "Without you? Didn't Remus say that you needed to keep me safe?"

"And I am, by getting you far from here. You're an asset to the Agency. Something they need and use to help guide their next move and gather intel. We have to keep you away from them."

She bristled. "Do you think I want to go back to them?" She pulled away and turned her back to him.

"No, I don't, but I also know that you don't want to be with the Syndicate. That's the only way to keep you safe if you stay. Have you become our asset, join us in our fight."

He was right, that wasn't something she wanted. "Then I guess I leave. Where are you taking me?" She tried to keep her voice from shaking.

"To a trusted friend, he'll teach you how to control your urges and help you get a new life. Once we're sure it's safe, you'll be able to leave and start your new life."

Away from him, without him. She wrapped her arms around herself and wondered why he was suddenly so important to her.

"Tell him," Krystal's voice came from her side. "Just tell him how you feel, and maybe he'll let you stay."

"I don't belong with the Syndicate. I don't want to be used." Lisa glanced over her shoulder to see if Alika had heard.

He lifted a brow, and she shook her head. "Don't worry about it."

"I am worried about it." He stood and wrapped his arms around her. "If you stayed, you could help us out, but Remus prefers his help to be willing. Not forced. Not like Romulus."

She shook her head. "I'm not the only medium in my family. Everyone wants to use us. Talk to their loved ones, find out who wronged someone else, spies. We moved out to the country because my parents couldn't take it anymore. They didn't want us to turn out like this."

"I hardly doubt they had a vampire in mind when they moved you all out to the country." He laughed. "But yeah, I see your point."

She thought back to how her parents thought it was going to be the best move for them. No one would know what they were; no one would bother them for favors or want to hire them for parties or investigations. She'd been ten when they moved, and she couldn't wait to get back to the city. "And it looks like I became what they feared."

He took her hand, and she turned to face him. "I would spare you from this. The Agency may not have killed you, but they took your life away from you. No one should have to suffer that."

She squeezed his hand and then let go. "This friend of yours. He'll be able to help me figure out a normal vampire life?"

"And he'll be able to keep you safe."

"Let's go see the house first and then take me to your friend." It'd probably be the last time she saw her home and her last chance to say goodbye to her family.

He walked passed her. "There are some more clothes for you in the bathroom; I'll let you get ready."

There was something in his voice that she couldn't recognize. "Thank you. I'll meet you upstairs in just a few minutes." After last night, she thought maybe he'd started to care for her. How silly.

Krystal was in the bathroom floating next to the clothes. "You are both being ridiculous. Would you just tell him you don't want to leave?"

"I don't want to be used by the Syndicate. Remus' brother has already used me enough. What's to stop Remus from doing the same thing?"

Krystal tapped her chin. "Oh, I don't know. He's more compassionate and isn't fucking insane?"

"I don't know that though." She shook her head. "I never should have moved back to the city. I should have lived at home like my parents wanted, and I should never have gone out for my birthday."

"Sometimes one mistake gives us the chance of a lifetime. If you would just talk to him. Let him know you care; then he wouldn't be breaking his own heart by sending you away."

Lisa raked her hands through her hair, tugging slightly. "Go away, don't you have other ghosts to talk to?"

"Nope. If you haven't noticed, I'm the only one around here." Krystal faded away. "But you know I'm right."

She didn't want to admit it, but the ghost probably had some points. But now was not the time to allow herself to get tangled with someone from the Syndicate, especially since she didn't know a whole lot about them.

She started the shower and stepped in. Could she tell Alika what she thought? Would it matter?

Alika walked around the living room as he sent a text to those in charge of securing Lisa's old house. He needed to make sure it was safe for them to go. It only took but a minute to get a reply back. It was safe for them both to show up, but he wasn't sure if he wanted her to go, safe or not. Closure, she wanted to see what had happened to her family and he couldn't blame her, but there could be an onslaught of emotions that she couldn't handle. And then she'd probably want to go after the Agency for revenge.

Which meant that she'd be in danger.

Unless he could get her to Tyson's without an issue, then she'd be Tyson's problem to restrain. A small bit of jealousy unfurled in his stomach. He didn't want Tyson near her while she was angry. He wanted to be the one to soothe her.

"Come on Alika, get it together."

"Are you talking to ghosts now too?" Her sweet voice drew his attention over to her.

Her wet hair stuck to her face slightly, and the black t-shirt clung to the curve of her body, blending into the black skinny jeans. He wanted to push her against the wall and have his way with her again. He rubbed his eyes. "I tried talking to Krystal last night; she always seemed to have advice."

"Yeah, I noticed that about her. Did you have any luck?" Her lip was turned up in a small smile, and he realized she was teasing him.

"Nope. You ready to go?"

The smile faded. "Yeah."

"Are you sure you want to do this? I don't want this to be the way you remember your family." Charred to unrecognizable corpses. A familiar pain laced through his chest as his memory conjured up images he didn't want to see. His own family still smoking from the fire at his home.

"I'm sure. I need to say my goodbyes before I start a new life." She came up and put a hand on his shoulder. "What is putting that look in your eyes?"

He shook his head. "Things I'd rather not say." He looked away from her and pulled up images in his mind of the farmhouse and willed his powers to take them there. When they reappeared, he steadied Lisa with a hand on her elbow. "I promise, you'll get used to it."

She chuckled. "Yeah, when I learn to do it on my own."

"You'll learn in time. I promise." He didn't look at the house but studied her. She was looking everywhere but the house.

Finally, she turned and faced the charred beams and scorched walls. He wondered what it was that she would see. Were the ghosts of her parents there? Did it work that way? He wanted to ask, but the moment he opened his mouth to say something she let out a heartbreaking sob.

He wrapped his arms around her, and she buried her face into his chest. They hadn't even gotten that close, and she was already in full grief, of course, she knew what was waiting for them. Just like he did. "You don't need to go further," he whispered. "You can say your goodbyes from here, let me hold you while you cry."

"No." She sniffled against him. "I need to see them. I need to talk to them."

He wasn't sure if there was a second meaning behind talk to them or not. "I'm right here with you."

She took a deep breath, and it was like she drew in all her pain and sorrow and just locked it away. Wiping her eyes, she moved towards the house with determined steps. He followed her, trying to figure out what to do to help her, but there was nothing he could think of, except be ready for whatever her reaction was going to be.

Lisa stepped away from Alika and walked toward the house. She didn't know who put the fire out or if it just ran out of usable fuel, but it didn't matter. It wasn't the bodies she was after; it was the spirits. The ghosts of her family she wanted to see and talk to.

The floor crunched and broke into ash under her feet, with smoke still coming up from embers below the surface. She just kept moving.

Her steps hesitated as she came to the ruins of the living room. There in the entryway skeletons leaned against each other, blackened by the fire. She put a hand to her mouth as bile rose in her throat.

She reached behind her to find Alika's hand, but he was gone. He'd promised he'd be right behind her. She looked around, starting to panic. When she turned back to face the house, he was standing in the entryway, his head bowed. She walked up to him and saw the tears on his cheek.

"Why do you cry?"

He took her hand and kissed it. "It's a nasty reminder. I know who sent the order out to kill your family."

"Romulus," a voice behind her said. She spun around to see a gray version of her sister standing there. "It was carried out by a woman who came to the house. She tied us up and set the house on fire."

Her heart broke. "Anya, I'm sorry. I'm so sorry."

"This wasn't your fault. You didn't lead them here. I don't know where you've been for the last five months, but I know you didn't want to bring this to us."

"They were trying to draw me out, send a message, make it seem like I had nowhere else to go, except back." Lisa hung her head. "I should have listened to mom and dad. I should have just stayed here."

"That's not true; they would have come anyway. The lady who came, mom and dad knew her."

Lisa's head shot up. "What?"

"You have to believe me, Lisa, there was a woman here, named Tara, she was one of mom's old friends."

Lisa saw red. "Tara was my handler." She snarled. "She did this?"

"She did. I don't know what happened exactly. We were all fine, just chatting, and Tara asked mom about you, if we'd seen you at all."

Lisa couldn't believe what she was hearing, "I'm going to murder her."

Anya continued, "She went on talking about how she heard you had a new job like she didn't know we reported you missing. The next thing I knew, everything had gone black. Then we woke up tied to each other, and the house was on fire."

"Please, don't tell me any more." She closed her eyes to focus on something else. This whole time she thought it had just been a random snatch, that she was just in the wrong place at the wrong time, but that wasn't it. Tara fucking knew who and what she was, but the bitch went along with the psychic theory that Romulus had about her. Why? Had Tara known she was going to be changed?

She opened her eyes, and Anya had faded away, replaced by Alika. "We're going back to the Agency," she told him.

"I don't think that's a wise idea. I'm going to get you to safety." He held his hand out to her. "You aren't thinking straight. You're crazy with grief."

She was, but that didn't matter to her. She wanted to tear into Tara's throat and drink the bitch dry. Alika wrapped his arms around her. "Listen to me, killing the agents isn't going to bring back your parents. You're a new vampire; you are no match for any of them."

Except for Tara, because the woman was always scared of her. An evil smile curled over her face, and she pulled Alika tight to her. "You're right." She closed her eyes, and he kissed her head.

"Hold on." He squeezed her, and she waited for the familiar feeling of the world around her shifting and changing. She'd expected him to take her to another safe house, but this was different. The noise of the city assaulted her ears, and it wasn't familiar. Her eyes darted around, and she looked up at the old brick house.

Her anger turned to sadness as she realized he really was going to leave her with someone else. "I don't want to go; please let me stay with you."

"Lisa, you can't. You don't belong with the Syndicate, not unless you want to be an asset, because that's how this life works." He kissed her head again, and she tried to stifle the tears that were forming.

"Remus doesn't need to know. I can just stay with you. I'll stay out of the way. I won't interfere. I…" her heart broke as she tried to find the words. "I don't want to be without you."

He tilted her chin and pressed his lips to hers. "You have to. Tyson… Tyson will take good care of you. He'll make sure that you learn how to hunt and feed and then help you with a new life."

That's not what she wanted anymore. She pulled away from his kiss. "I don't want this."

"I want you safe. I'm not safe; the Syndicate is not safe." He reached and knocked on the door.

She wrapped her arms around herself trying to block out the sounds of the city and not focus on the fact that he was abandoning her to a stranger.

An olive-skinned man opened the door, he barely stood taller than her, and his dark eyes pegged her, and he smirked. "You're going to owe me one for this, Alika."

"Nice to see you too Tyson. This is Lisa."

Lisa raised a small hand. "Hi, I hear that I'm your problem now."

"She's a little bitter." Alika sighed. "I'm sorry."

Tyson shook his head. "Don't be, we all know that this is best. Did you get her fed?"

"I don't need to eat." She shook her head. "I'm not hungry." There was no hunger going through her right now, just a flood of emotions bouncing between disappointment, anger, and heartbreak. Of course, this wasn't a fairy tale, and just because she slept with Alika didn't mean that they were meant to be.

Tyson stepped aside and waved them in. "She's pretty young to have that kind control."

"Long story, but she'll have to tell you if she wants. Just keep an eye on her."

Lisa didn't glance back at him; it didn't matter what he was saying. What mattered was the thirteen people, ghosts, that stood in front of her. They had the same features as Tyson, with just slightly different faces and heights, and there was one woman with long hair.

They all stared at her silently as if trying to assess what she was. "Um, hello," she said softly, trying not to draw Tyson's or Alika's attention to her.

Alika looked over Tyson's shoulder where Lisa was standing in the living room. The woman uttered a small hello, and he wondered who she was meeting now. "I'm sorry Tyson, for disrupting your life."

"It's alright General. I'll get her taught and on her own in no time. Are you sure you're okay with this?"

Alika squared his shoulders and nodded. "I'm fine with it." Though there was an ache in his chest that was saying otherwise. "However, I think I know how to fix all of this."

"All of this?" Tyson glanced back at Lisa. "Who is she talking to?"

"Spirits, ghosts, whatever is lurking in your living room. And yes, she's not happy with me, but if I can make things a little safer for her, then she can come back."

Tyson shook his head. "And what about the Syndicate? They'll want her abilities. I thought you wanted to keep her far away from that."

"Maybe if I make it clear to Remus that she's off limits."

"Has she met the man?"

Alika nodded. "Yeah, she had a message to deliver to him."

"Yeah, then you know he's not going to let her go."

He hated that his friend was right on that. If Remus thought Lisa would be useful, then he'd find a way to make her work for them, and it wasn't like he could just leave the Syndicate. "Yeah, you're right. You know I can't come back then, yeah?"

Tyson nodded. "Don't worry man; I've got this. She'll be on her own and hunting like a pro in a few months. Found a nest of vampires overseas that might be willing to take her in."

As long as it wasn't in an area known for Agency sympathy, she'd be fine. "That would be perfect for her." He turned to leave.

"Aren't you at least going to say goodbye?"

Alika shook his head. "No, because if I do, I might not leave." He disappeared off the step of the house and reappeared in his own home. He may not be able to stay with her, but he knew what he could do. Kill Tara and deliver her body to Lisa.

He walked over the empty living room and went downstairs to where his real home was. It was larger than the safe house, even though he didn't need the room. The bedroom took up the majority of the layout since he didn't need a kitchen downstairs, but he walked past that into a small room at the end of the hall. His weapons room.

He wasn't sure what Tara was, but it didn't matter, chopping off the head of most creatures would kill them. He didn't know where to find her, but he knew that he could draw the bitch out.

He pulled out his phone and called the main line for the Agency. He waited until someone picked up.

"Agency Operator, how can I direct your call?" The woman's voice was way too chipper for his liking.

"Yes, I have a message for a woman named Tara. I believe she works in the intelligence department." He kept his voice even.

The woman on the other line hesitated. "Sir, Tara doesn't take phone calls—"

"Tell her it's in concern of a woman named Lisa Thorne. She'll take my call."

"Erm, please hold."

There was a click, and then the elevator music started. Every few seconds a recorded message would play ranging from 'your call is important to us' to 'The Agency: Making the world safer for all creatures.'

He rolled his eyes each time a recorded message came on and was about to give up when the line clicked again. "Agent Jade speaking."

"Hello, Agent Jade. I've heard that you've misplaced your asset, Lisa Thorne."

"Perhaps, what's in it for you?"

He smirked knowing that he had her. "Your boss must be pretty pissed that you let a medium go free."

"Not the point. What information on her do you have?"

"She's with me. Still blood-starved because she's refusing to eat. Want her back? It'll cost you." He traced his hand over the dull side of a sword. It was going to cost her a lot more than she expected.

There was a rustling on the other side of the phone, and then she finally sighed. "Name your price."

"Ten grand and you meet me down in the drug district."

There was more hesitation in her voice. "That's Syndicate territory."

"No, not all of it. There's a warehouse towards the center that the human druggies have managed to keep as theirs. Know it?" He brushed the handle of his sword and imagined the force it would take to strike through Tara's neck. All for the sake of Lisa.

"Meet me there at midnight?"

"Perfect." He disconnected the call. The woman wasn't stupid, of course, he needed to be prepared if he was walking into a trap. He sent a quick message to William and knew the wolf would have his back.

It was time to kill an agent.

CHAPTER SIX

Lisa stood in the living room staring at the silent ghosts. She'd never not had one talk back to her, at the very least, question what she was. These didn't even do that. They faded away the moment Tyson came up behind her.

"How long can you go without feeding?"

"I don't really know." She shook her head. "When I was in isolation I didn't have a way of telling time. I've only been out for a few days." A few wonderful days with Alika, and now her future was looking as bleak as ever.

"Isolation, great. Okay." Tyson moved so he was in front of her and one of the ghosts appeared next to him, talking in a language she couldn't understand.

She shook her head. "I don't speak that language."

Tyson let out a frustrated sigh. "I'm speaking English."

"Sorry, I wasn't talking to you. What were you saying? I couldn't hear you." She met his gaze and saw the confusion. "There's a man next to you, he looks a lot like you, but he's speaking in a foreign language."

Tyson pinched the bridge of his nose. "Right, ghosts, spirits. I'm not sure I want to know who that is."

The ghosts next to him opened his mouth and started screaming. She resisted covering her ears. "I...I need..." She tried to focus, what had helped this last time? "Headphones, music."

"I've got an mp3 player you can borrow. Tomorrow night we'll go to the store and get you one of your own." But it was Alika that was supposed to do that for her, not Tyson. She tried to remind herself that Alika left her here and that she needed to move on.

The other ghosts appeared and started screaming at her as well. She covered her ears and tried not to fall to her knees. "I don't understand what you're saying."

"Can you repeat it to me?" Tyson put a hand on her shoulder, and she pulled away from him.

She stumbled through the words. Tyson nodded. "I've got it. They're warning you. Damn it. Do ghosts just talk to each other or what?"

They stopped screaming the moment he said he got it. She looked at him and slowly lowered her hands. "Yes, they do. What kind of warning was it?"

"The love of your life is about to do something extremely stupid. He's going after Tara, and it's going to be a massive trap."

Her eyes widened. "Why would he do that?"

"Probably to give you some sort of revenge." Tyson shrugged. "Hell if I know."

She paced the living room. She had to get there first. She couldn't allow Tara to kill him. She looked at Tyson. "I need you to take me to wherever Alika is."

"Nope, my job is to keep you safe, and I want nothing to do with this battle." He sat down on his couch and crossed his arms. "Sorry baby vampire, you're staying here."

Except she couldn't. She needed to stop Alika. She'd transported herself a couple times before. Small distances, but maybe if she focused she could take herself back to the safe house. That would be a good place to start. Or she could take herself right to Alika.

She opened her mouth to ask Tyson how the transportation worked and he held up a hand.

"I'm not teaching you anything right now that can get you in trouble."

Well, it would have been worth a shot. Something curled inside her, calling to her, and she tilted her head to the side. A craving that came up only when she started to feel the need to feed.

A craving for Romulus' blood. She licked her lips, brushing the tip of her fangs. She could recall him perfectly. The taste of his blood, the way that it filled the craving in her body.

She closed her eyes and moaned at the thought of tasting it again, and she wanted it. She needed it.

Lisa opened her eyes and was standing in an office she'd never seen before. Standing right in front of Romulus and Tara.

"Shit," she whispered, and the moment she opened her mouth to speak all the ghosts screamed. This wasn't the Agency building, this was something else entirely, a new set of ghosts that only screamed wordlessly.

Romulus appeared in front of her and grabbed her by the hair. "Thought you were with our mysterious phone caller."

"I don't know what you're talking about." She tried to cover her ears, but Tara came up behind her and cuffed her wrists.

Tara jerked her away from Romulus. "We got a call saying someone had you. Looks like it was a trap." She laughed. "But it looks like we now have the perfect bait."

She'd made a grave mistake. Romulus walked up to her and touched her cheek. "No control, new vampire, and addicted to a demigod's blood. You stupid, stupid girl."

She turned her face and snapped at his hand. "You made me into this monster."

He jerked his hand away. "You're right, and you're at my mercy because you'll never be fully satisfied without feeding from me. Take her with you; it'll be leverage for whoever is coming."

It would be Alika. She'd screwed over his plan, and now there was nothing she could do about it. Except. She looked around to see if any of the spirits would listen to her instead of scream at her.

One stood there silently, staring at her. "Warn him. Somehow," she whispered. The ghost nodded and faded away.

Tara jerked. "What are you rambling on about now?"

"You killed my family. You bitch. You knew me all along. Why me?"

"Because you were the most likely to fall into a trap. You wanted out of that farmhouse so bad. Your mother told me you ran off to live in the city. I sent the vampire to the bar that night to change you." She laughed. "My pretending I didn't know what you were kept you off guard, kept you confused and weak." She shoved her towards the door. "Let's go, we have a hot date at midnight, and I don't want to be late."

Alika looked around the empty lot of the warehouse. Nothing seemed out of place, nothing moved in the shadows, but William was waiting in the wings just in case.

A car pulled up, and he recognized the sleek black look and tinted windows. Tara. Except there was another person in the car; he could see the outline of the head. No, no way. He sensed it though. Lisa was in the car with her.

What the ever loving hell? What stupid thing did that woman do now?

Tara got out of the car, pulling Lisa with her. "Look what I found. She came begging for some of Romulus' blood."

"Get out. It's a trap." Lisa screamed, but Tara cupped a hand over her mouth. "Looks like the asset is mine now and you can just… die." She held a hand up and clicked her fingers; several vampires appeared, all holding AK-47s.

"Just another bloodsucker dying over a turf war." Tara jerked Lisa. "Romulus is considering having her as his personal medium now, keeping her by his side and feeding her blood only when she gives him proper information."

Like leading on a druggy with their addiction. He couldn't let that happen to her. He took a step forward, and Tara shook her head. "Not another step or they'll open fire."

His foot barely twitched before bullets started flying around the lot. Tara dragged Lisa with her as the new vampire kicked and struggled to get out of the woman's grip, screaming for him.

She wasn't getting away with this. He transported himself to the car, but the moment he reached for Lisa, a bullet took him in the chest. She looked back and cried out for him, even with the cuffs she managed to transport herself out of Tara's grip about a foot away.

She ran to him, but another bullet took her in the side, knocking her away from him.

"Go," he ground out. He looked around; there had to be ghosts here. Had to be. "Tell her to go. Tell her about Will." Another bullet pierced his knee.

Lisa suddenly looked up, her wide eyes turned to him, and she nodded as Tara pulled her back to her feet and shoved her into the car.

"Tell her I'll come get her," he whispered. "Make her understand."

The world around him started going black as pain laced through his body. Vampire or not, several bullet wounds were going to take its toll on him and eventually bring him to death. Except he had a cheeky werewolf hidden away.

Lisa sat in the car as it drove, her head held down as the pain in her side started to spread through her body. What was it that Alika had said would keep a wound from healing? Silver.

"Can't you take the bullet out?" She groaned. "I came back to you. It fucking hurts."

Tara shook her head. "I'm not getting your blood on my hands. You can suffer for a while."

Lisa ground her teeth and looked out the window. If what Tara had been saying were true, Lisa expected her to take them either back to isolation or Romulus' office. But the road they were on took them in the opposite direction of both. "Where are we going?"

"There's a scene I need you to look at, just on the edge of town. We'll be staying there for the day."

Panic pulled at Lisa's stomach as she tried to imagine what kind of scene would take her all day to investigate. Especially now that she was mostly fed and better able to concentrate. "What kind of scene?"

"There was a mass killing of twenty low-level agents. We believe the Syndicate is behind it. You'll tell us if they were and name them for us."

She shook her head. "Mass graves are hard to tell the voices apart. Do we know how they were killed?" Maybe if she played along, she'd have a better chance of surviving to figure out how she was going to get back to Alika.

"Torture." There was something in her voice that Lisa found odd.

What on earth was she going to do with a room full of tortured ghosts? If she were lucky, she'd get a name from them, but they could all revert back to their death scenes at any time, and she wasn't sure if she had the stomach for that or not. They might all refuse to talk to her.

She pulled her knees up on the seat and laid her head on them. If only she could get out of the cuffs and travel to Alika again. But with her luck, she'd end up right back wherever Romulus was again.

"Regretting everything? You've had a taste of freedom, and now you'll go back to your lonely isolation chamber. With no chance of escape again, because trust me, I won't make that mistake again."

Lisa looked out the window as the city started to thin out a bit. She didn't answer because deep down she knew that Tara was right. She regretted leaving her isolation room because now she knew that she could be a functioning vampire, that her family wouldn't have shunned her, that she could have a life with Alika. And now, that was all being ripped away from her again.

She closed her eyes and tried to reach out to anyone, part of her felt Alika, but she was sure that was her mind playing tricks on her.

Thirty minutes and the car finally came to a stop. She jerked as Tara pulled her out of the car. Pausing, Lisa took in the scene in front of her. A giant airplane hangar took up most of her view, and she turned to face Tara. The large garage-like door was shut, and there was a regular door to the left of that. "What on earth?"

"What were you expecting? A nice house?"

"There are fifty ghosts standing there." She studied all of them, most of them were in street clothes, some wore suits, both genders, all just standing there staring at her. They weren't agency. They were Syndicate. She turned to run, and Tara grabbed her by the hair. "You're going to do this. I want to know everything that happened here."

"These are Syndicate ghosts; you can't tell me that you don't know that the Agency killed them." She tried to pull away, but the pain in her head became too much.

Tara smiled, and she walked through the door of the airplane hangar, shoving Lisa along, ignoring the stumbling Lisa was doing. "Perhaps this isn't about information as much as it's about torture." Tara turned and locked the door behind them.

The moment the door closed, all the ghosts started screaming at her. The noise made her head explode as she begged them to stop. They couldn't do this to her. They had to understand. She couldn't handle all the voices.

She wished for Alika to appear and put headphones over her ears to drown out the screaming voices. The ghosts continued their unintelligent screaming until a shrill voice went through them.

"She's not Agency."

The voices died down into a murmur of questioning as they searched for who the new voice belonged to. Lisa lifted her gaze to see what was going on. Krystal stood there walking through the ghost crowd. "She's not Agency. She's not Syndicate either."

Lisa's eyes darted to Tara to see how much she could risk speaking. Tara was leaning against the wall, checking her phone, not paying attention to the scene. "I need help," she whispered.

One of the ghosts faded away only to reappear a few feet in front of her, chained to the ground as someone stripped the skin from them. White noise took the place of the words the torturer was saying, but Lisa had a feeling it was a demand for information.

Bile rose in her throat as she could see the blood pouring from the skin. The poor person screamed and jerked as the Agent continued. Another ghost faded away, and Lisa looked around to see where they reappeared.

Tied to something against the wall, the man screamed as a shadowed Agent approached him, a branding iron in his hand, heated up and glowing red. She turned away before he could shove the metal into his victim.

"I need Alika," she whispered. "I don't want to watch this."

Krystal disappeared as more scenes of torture started to appear, and the ghosts' screams echoed through the airplane hangar. She was going to go insane before Tara let her out of here.

Alika woke up, staring into William's wide eyes. The familiar taste of blood coated his tongue, and he slowly sat up. The last thing he remembered was asking a ghost to help Lisa and a spray of bullets. He was lucky nothing shredded his heart or that an agent didn't try to take his head.

"You were right to call me for backup, but dude, even in wolf form I wasn't going to be able to take that many agents."

Alida looked over a healing wound on his chest. "Yeah, I didn't expect you to. You did exactly what I wanted, you got me out of there, fed, and starting to heal. Do we know where that bitch took Lisa?"

William was silent and looked away.

"William?" Alika prompted. "Where is Lisa?"

He shook his head. "I don't know. Skye checked the Agency system, and she hasn't been checked back into isolation."

His heart fell, was Tara telling the truth then? The idea of Lisa being Romulus' pet vampire filled him with enough anger he thought about actually going after the demigod. He could rip his head off and then it'd be done. Everything would be done. No more war without the leader.

Except, Romulus would kill him on sight. He needed to know where Lisa was in order to save her, but he also needed to know what he'd be walking into.

He closed his eyes and tried to get any sense of her at all. She was another vampire, he wasn't her maker, but he should still be able to get an idea of where she was. There was a small hint of something, but he wasn't sure where it came from, but at least he knew that she was alive.

He looked at William. "I need to know any places that the Agency might need to gather information, especially violent places. Something that might need a medium."

"I'll see what I can find out. Talk to Zeek? Maybe he has a list since he's the computer guy?"

He shook his head. "I need you to talk to him. I have something else that I need to handle right now. I need to talk to Remus."

"And tell him what?" William shook his head. "Remus isn't going to care about Lisa, not unless she's going to work for him."

He nodded. "I know, but that's not what I'm going to go talk to him about." No, he had something else in mind entirely. He went to the bathroom to clean himself up.

He'd made it his mission in life to take down the Agency and dethrone Romulus, but now he had something else much more important to protect, and if it meant giving up his connections to the Syndicate, he would. Lisa didn't belong in the war, and maybe it was time for him to step down from it.

He finished cleaning up and then took himself to the Starlight Lounge where he knew Remus would be enjoying the show and very possibly enjoying the company of one of Nova's sirens.

The club was full of people at tables with their eyes trained on the stage where a woman was singing at the mic. He didn't know who she was, so he didn't pay any attention to her. He focused on making his way back to the VIP section where Remus would be.

The bouncer at the section didn't bother him as he walked in. Remus, however, lifted a brow. "What are you doing here?"

"I've come to ask to leave the Syndicate." He kept his voice even. "Once

I've secured Lisa from the Agency, I want to leave and start over with her."

Remus leaned forward, his arms on the table. "I don't think you understand; there is no leaving the Syndicate. Not unless you're dead."

He was afraid that was going to be the answer. "I'd still be protecting something the Agency wants, but she doesn't belong in this war."

"Then she should have figured out how to avoid the Agency, shouldn't she? You bring her back, and you convince her to become our asset. I've decided she's too valuable to just return to the normal world."

This wasn't exactly how he was expecting the talk to go. "She doesn't want to be an asset."

"Give her an ultimatum then. She stays with you, becomes our asset, or we kill her so that the Agency can't have her."

He locked his jaw. "I don't think that's a good idea."

"I don't care. You are part of my mafia, my Syndicate; you will do as I tell you or I'll make sure Zeek hands out an appropriate consequence."

Which probably meant death or torture. He didn't say anything, and Remus smiled.

"I see we have a deal, good, now go. You're interrupting the show."

Alika nodded and took himself back to his house where William was sitting on the couch patiently waiting.

"Remember a couple years ago when we lost fifty lower Syndicate agents?"

Alika nodded slowly. "Yes, why?"

"She's there, one of our scouts went and checked it out, her scent is there, and she's screaming."

Tara was torturing her. "That bitch is dead."

CHAPTER SEVEN

Lisa slowly lifted her head and looked through the hair that was falling over her face. The scenes were starting to fade and the voices with them. Out of habit, she took a deep breath to calm herself. It wouldn't be long until the ghosts returned and the scenes of torture continued.

It was enough to drive anyone mad. Even her. Her body ached from tensing through all the screaming; the cuffs bit into her wrists as she tried to pull them out to cover her ears. Blood tears streaked down her cheeks as she begged it to end. Tara was nowhere in sight right now, and Lisa couldn't sense or hear her.

She closed her eyes and pictured Alika, how he held her and cared about the overwhelming voices that she heard. How he found a solution she would never have thought of. Music. Loud, beat-heavy music. The whisper of voices started up again, trickling their way to a roar. She opened her eyes and started singing at the top of her lungs.

The voices raised above hers and she continued to sing. It was the only thing she could think of to do to help drown everything out, but it wasn't working. Screams for help, screams of tortured victims, words she couldn't make out. It was all so much that she started to succumb to the mental exhaustion of it all.

A small little voice rose up above the rest, barely audible, like a whisper in the wind. "He's coming."

But that was impossible. Alika wouldn't know where she was. How to get there. Hell, she barely knew where she was, not to mention she had almost gotten him killed. Guilt hit her hard as she thought about the number of bullets that had hit him. Her side ached at the reminder that there was one still in her. Her skin had healed over it, trapping it in her muscle, but it was still there causing pain.

But the voice came again. "He's coming." She let herself believe that he was because if she didn't, she would have lost all hope.

"Please, Alika, please," she whispered before starting to sing at the top of her lungs again.

Alika appeared near the airplane hangar. Nothing moved around it. Where was Tara? He shook his head and thanked whatever deity he could that the hangar was unguarded. He tilted his head at the sound that he heard though.

Lisa, not screaming as the scout had said, but singing at the top of her lungs. He imagined she was trying to keep her sanity. He took a step forward but ducked back behind a tree when a car pulled up to the hangar. Tara walked out, and the car drove off.

The woman scoffed as she walked up to the hangar and opened the door to the side of the huge one meant for airplanes. Alika crept forward and paused at the still cracked door. He looked in to see Tara grabbing the now silent Lisa by the hair.

"Romulus needs you now."

"Fuck him," Lisa spat out.

"He thought that might be your answer; he'll feed you if you do this for him."

He saw Lisa hesitate. He held his breath to watch how she reacted. "No."

Tara pulled out a knife, and before Alika could see what her intentions were, he drew a throwing knife from his boot and flicked it at Tara, nailing her lower back with it. The woman spun around and ripped the knife out.

Her features started to change a bit, and Alika realized what he was dealing with. A mother fucking changeling. He should have been able to know that after encountering her in the isolation level. He had no idea how he'd missed the strange smell they normally carried. He snarled as her features turned to Lisa's.

"You wouldn't hurt me, would you?" Even her voice sounded like Lisa's. She threw the knife away and started to sway toward him. "You want to save me, take me away from this place."

Lisa snarled and threw herself to the ground, swinging her legs around to catch Tara's ankles. Tara fell to the ground but pulled a gun out from a holster hidden in her pants. She shot at Lisa, but the shot went wild.

Alika rushed toward her, drawing his two curved blades from the sheath on his back. All he needed was a clear shot at cutting her head off. Lisa wasn't going to be much help with her hands pinned behind her back, so he was going to have to watch out for her.

Tara flipped to her feet and changed back to her first appearance. He hadn't gone up against a changeling before, and he wasn't sure what this tiny creature was going to be able to do to him. He had her on speed, strength, and size.

She flicked her wrists, and her hands turned to claws. What the actual fuck? He blinked a few times as she rushed towards him and started slashing at him madly. He jumped back, dodging her wild hands. Her speed matched his, and he had a clear view of how they managed to hold their own in the supernatural world.

He growled as her claw caught his shirt and left a trail of blood on his chest. If he wasn't careful, she could cut him to shreds.

A wild scream came through the hangar, and both him and Tara stopped for a moment and looked over at Lisa. She'd gotten the cuffs off her hands some-how and was now covering her ears screaming like a banshee.

Tara laughed. "She's going insane from the ghosts. They all want her to help them; they've been screaming at her and reliving their torture."

He transported himself to her. "Lisa? Lisa!" He grabbed her shoulders and shook her a little bit.

Lisa raised her eyes to him, and they weren't the same big round eyes he'd seen before. Now he could see the terror in them, her lids rimmed with red from crying. There was no laughter or light to them. "Lisa listen to me." He tried to pull her hands down. She resisted and shook her head slowly.

Her hands fell to her side, and her gaze moved away from him and to behind him. "No!"

He thought she was telling him no, but a moment later he looked down to see pale blue claws sticking out of his chest. He'd been stupid and taken his eyes off Tara, all to try and bring Lisa back from the edge of madness.

He heard Tara laughing from behind him. "You stupid, stupid vampire."

Lisa saw Alika grab his chest as Tara pulled her claws out of him. She had no idea what Tara was, but at the moment, her world narrowed down to that bitch. Despite the ghosts screaming at her and the sounds of torture surrounding her, the only thing she could focus on was Tara. She stood and grabbed Alika's blades.

She held the slightly curved knives up and smiled; she knew exactly what she needed to do. Tara's eyes went wide. "You're too weak to kill me."

"You think so?" Lisa moved forward. "I just broke my thumbs to get out of your silver cuffs, and they've healed already." That had been a gamble on her part, but it had worked. "My skin has healed over the silver bullet." Though it still hurt like hell, adrenaline was carrying her through the moment. She'd take time to tend to herself and Alika once the bitch was dead.

Lisa focused on Tara and willed herself to appear in front of the woman. To her surprise, it happened, and she sliced down with one of the blades. Tara jumped back and looked down at the torn blouse.

Lisa smiled. So she moved just as quick, that was good to know. Claws and speed were the woman's only defenses that she could see. Lisa however, had two swords, strength, and a thirst for blood.

She licked her lips and lunged at the woman. Tara hit one of Lisa's wrists with the heel of her hand. Lisa cried out as her hand went numb and the blade flew across the room. She brought the other one straight across, cutting Tara's stomach. It wasn't deep enough to be harmful, but the blood dripped down, catching Lisa's eye.

Her tongue darted out between her fangs, and she launched herself towards Tara, discarding the knife. All she wanted was blood. Nothing else mattered. Tara claws dragged across Lisa's face, but the pain didn't cause her to hesitate. She grabbed the woman's wrist and used it to yank Tara to her.

Lisa grinned as she bared her fangs and bit into Tara's neck. The changeling cried out, and Lisa shoved her to the ground, pinning Tara with her body. Her teeth never let go of the neck as she drank in the sweet blood. The taste was sweeter than the werewolf's, but not as delicious as Romulus' blood. It didn't matter though, the craving inside her didn't care what flavor it was, all it needed was to be fed.

Tara's claws dragged down her back, ripping the back of her shirt to shreds. This time, Lisa pulled back a bit, just in time for Tara's elbow to meet her jaw. She jerked back and growled. Tara snarled at her, baring tiny fangs.

A laugh bubbled out of Lisa's mouth at the thought of those tiny little fangs compared to hers. Tara reared back and bit into Lisa's collarbone. She screamed and scrambled backward, the teeth tearing a chunk of flesh from her shoulder. They might have been tiny, but they hurt like a bitch.

Tara got up to her feet, stumbling some as she did. Lisa noted the weakness and felt behind her for one of the knives. Her fingers met the leather-wrapped hilt, and she wrapped her hand around it, watching Tara struggle to get her bearings.

The changeling fell to her knees and cursed. Lisa got up and transported herself over to Tara, raising the blade above her head. "Down with the bitch," she whispered and let the blade drop, the momentum carrying it through the bone and flesh of the changeling.

Lisa stumbled back as the head hit the floor and rolled toward Alika. Her vampire stood, still holding a hand to his chest where he'd been stabbed, but the blood was slowing now.

Lisa looked at him and then to Tara. "I…she…I…" Even the ghosts were silent right now.

"She was evil and needed to be dealt with. You did the right thing."

But she'd taken a life in a blind rage. Her body shook a little, and Alika wrapped his arms around her. "Shh, it's okay. You're safe now. We're safe now. Let's get home and tend to our wounds."

Because her back was torn to shreds and there was a silver bullet in her side still, and he'd been stabbed. They'd heal, and quickly, but she knew there was a choice to make about Alika and the Syndicate.

She looked up at him, and he kissed her gently. "I am so proud of you."

The ghosts started murmuring again, but before they could start screaming, Alika took her away.

They reappeared in a different home, and she glanced around. Similar to the safe house they had been in, the upstairs was almost completely untouched, so she figured there was more in the basement. "Where are we?"

"Home." Alika took her hand and pulled her toward the stairs. "Let's get cleaned up and rested. Tomorrow night we can deal with the question I know that's on your mind."

She snorted a little, but let him pull her toward the stairs. "And what do you think is the question on my mind?"

"What comes next." He sighed and turned to face her. "I shouldn't have left you with Tyson. I should have kept you with me and convinced you that being an asset to the Syndicate would be the best way for you to go because I want to keep you with me."

"I told you that I didn't want to be part of the Syndicate and you sent me away." She shook her head. "But I see now that I can't not be a part of this war. Both sides know I exist, both sides know what I am capable of." She looked to her side where she saw a ghost of a woman and two small boys, and she realized who they were. His family, they followed him everywhere, even if their spirits weren't solid. "He's all alone."

The woman nodded and motioned to him. "He's all yours. Take care of him. Someone has to."

"Who are you talking to?" He glanced at where she was staring. "Who's here?"

Lisa smiled. "Your wife and two sons, they are beautiful."

She saw his face crumple, and she put a hand on his cheek. "She doesn't blame you; she's been watching over you. It's time to let them go so they can be free. They aren't tied to where they died. They're tied to you."

He took a deep breath and kissed her. "I love you. Since the moment I saw you, I knew there was something different about you."

She returned the kiss, wrapping her hand around his neck to draw him further in. "I love you too. Thank you, for coming to my rescue."

She glanced as the ghosts faded away, all three of them smiling. He wrapped an arm around her, and she winced as it hit the bullet in her side. "That's going to be a bitch to get out. Isn't it?"

"Oh yeah, but really, after taking on a changeling's claws, I think you'll be all right." He chuckled and led her downstairs.

She looked over the massive room and smiled. "I could get used to this, lots of space."

He led her to the weapons room and pulled out a cloth to clean the blades. "I'll teach you to fight, you may become an asset, but we always need more people on the field. I won't leave you defenseless." He slowly wiped down the blades, removing all trace of blood before putting them back where they belonged.

She nodded and traced her hand over a compacted bow. "I'd love to learn. I was never one for fighting, but this is a new life."

He kissed her forehead. "And I'm happy to help you with that." He chuckled. "Now, time to get cleaned up."

CHAPTER EIGHT

Two weeks later, Alika pulled Lisa into the office building of the Syndicate. She didn't hesitate in putting in her earbuds and letting the loud music drown out the ghosts here. It was something she was getting used to, having the music help her keep her sanity.

He'd helped get her blood cravings under control with the help of William, but there was nothing she could do about the voices. His house was quiet, but their city was a violent one, and it seemed no matter where they went there was a ghost or ten screaming at her.

Once she got used to the music and they found a volume she could still carry a conversation on with, she settled down more. Less screaming back at the ghosts and more outgoing. Keeping her fed was proving critical as she still had a craving for Romulus' blood if she became too hungry.

They walked into Remus' office, and Lisa gave a little wave to the seemingly empty room.

"I see she's still talking to ghosts, that's good." Remus' voice came from behind them.

She spun around and glared at him, but Alika put a hand on her shoulder. "Yes, and it's not just going to go away. She has something to tell you."

"Oh, this should be fun." Remus gestured with his hand. "Get on with it."

She crossed her arms. "I'm agreeing to come on as an asset."

"Yeah, you didn't really have a choice in that." He laughed. "Did you think you did?"

"Well, here's the thing, I'm the one who talks to ghosts. You want me to give you correct information, you better as hell at least pretend that I have a choice."

Remus' brows shot up, and he glanced at Alika. "Found her voice, has she?"

He nodded. "Just listen."

"I want to be paid for the work I do; I'm not free, I'm not a slave, I'm not a forced worker. I'm a medium, a vampire, and soon I'll be one hell of a fighter. There will be no withholding feedings from me, no locking me up. I want the freedom I've had since being with Alika."

His heart swelled. He knew she wanted to stay with him, but he hadn't really realized what her fears were when it came to being an asset. In her mind, the Syndicate and Agency were on the same level.

Remus snarled. "What the hell kind of person do you think I am?"

Lisa took a step back, and her confidence shrank a little.

"I don't torture those who willing help me out. I wouldn't strip you of your freedoms unless you betrayed the Syndicate or me." His look softened a little bit. "Whatever monster you think I am, I'm not. My cruelty has limits, whereas my brother's does not."

Lisa relaxed, and Alika bowed his head. "Thank you, that's all she needed to know."

"Now go, enjoy your new life together. I'll call on you when I need you."

Alika led her out with an arm around her shoulder. "See it wasn't that bad." He chuckled, and she elbowed him lightly in the stomach. "Come on, you heard the new boss, let's enjoy our new life, together."

LOST IT ALL
Mia Bishop

CHAPTER ONE

"Sam." The dark figure detached from the shadows and kept pace as Sam continued to make his way through the busy street. Hands shoved in his pockets, head down to avoid the rain, he moved deftly, making sure to avoid obstacles, and he knew the man following him would do the same. "Samuel, I have a favor to ask."

Sam kept his pace steady but looked over his shoulder, eyeing the confectioner's box in the man's hand. "A favor?"

"Can we talk?"

Sam stopped, turning slowly to face his shadow. "It's pouring out here, meet me at the bookstore in an hour. We can talk there."

The man smiled, and as if on cue, the rain stopped. A shaft of sunlight illuminated a strand of silver hair peeking out from the bowler hat perched on the man's head. "Are you on the hunt right now?"

"Bast sent me out with a lead." He gave a sideways glance around him and leaned closer. "We found the killer."

"You'll need your strength; it's a good thing I come bearing gifts." He held out the white box tied with a blue ribbon. "You need to stop taking orders from that man. You have the eyes of a king; you should be a leader."

"He's our leader, not me. I have to take orders from him." Sam pushed his hood back and ran his hands through his hair, pushing the strands out of his eyes. "And my eyes are those of a hunter, not a king." Rem snorted in disagreement, but Sam ignored it. To the best of his knowledge, not even Rem knew the truth; the old man simply had a hunch. Sam nodded toward a nearby alley and walked a few feet in before turning to his companion. "Gift or bribe?"

The man's lip twitched. "I should think a bribe wouldn't be necessary."

Sam rubbed the back of his neck. "Sorry, Rem, I didn't mean—"

"No apologies, son. Everyone is on edge lately."

Sam bowed his head slightly to show the man who'd saved him from starvation as a teenager the respect he was due. "The Agency rousted one of our clubs last week. I don't even know how they found out about it. We keep a low profile. They destroyed our supplies. Luckily they never made it back to file a report, or we'd be shut down." Sam's blue eyes looked up to find Rem grinning. "Did you have something to do with the agent's car accident?"

"I protect what's important to me, Sam."

"So, this favor, what is it?"

"A simple mission."

"The debt I owe you for saving me. Anything you need, you know I'll do it."

"You don't owe me anything. Your survival was payment enough. And over the past ninety years, you've repaid that debt a million times over." He shifted his gaze to make sure no one passing by on the nearby busy street was paying any attention to them and continued, "but this favor is of the utmost importance."

"Okay. What's the job?"

Rem's voice turned dark. "Just outside the wolves' warehouses in the waterfront is an Agency shipping yard, small, unmarked, very discreet in appearance. Inside is a cargo container. I need it opened, and I need the items inside safely returned, but," he paused, "there's one item in particular that I need secured."

"What's the item?"

Rem held out a picture. Sam hesitated but finally took it. Big blue doe-eyes stared back at him, framed by long strands of brown hair, a pert little nose, and plump pink lips. He swallowed down the unfamiliar feeling of anxiety bubbling up. His gut twisted into a knot, and it wasn't from hunger; something about the woman in the picture was turning him inside out. As a cold sweat beaded his forehead, he managed three words with barely any voice left to speak them, "Who is she?"

There was no answer. Sam looked up, but Rem was gone. Vanished without a trace. Typical of his savior. He turned the picture over and found a name scrawled on the back. "Malia," he whispered.

Shoving the picture into his back pocket, he tugged his hood up as the rain started up again and headed towards his original destination. He fought the urge to take off after the woman. His fingers itched to find the shipping container and rip the doors from the hinges, but he needed a cool head for this mission. If it were important to Rem, then Sam would take every measured precaution to make sure he succeeded. He knew deep down it had less to do with Rem and more to do with the woman in the picture; he would succeed to make sure she was safe. Whoever she was, she wasn't just important to Rem, she was calling to his soul, and he would find her.

His stomach cramped, a sharp reminder of his primary goal at the moment. Food. Untying the blue ribbon, Sam inhaled the sweet metallic scent as he fished out the fresh delicacy Rem had given him. Popping the chewy morsel into his mouth, he slowly chewed as he continued on his path. Sam ducked his head to avoid the gazes of any passersby and made his way to the location Bast had given him. As he stood outside of the apartment, his mouth watered. Sam's smooth teeth started to transform into razor sharp weapons, and from the haze of red coloring his vision, he knew his eyes had changed as well. Normally he'd refuse to feed from someone who hadn't consented, he had his regulars to keep him well fed most of the time, but this man was a special case.

Sam's lips curled into a menacing grin. He turned the door handle to find it locked. The feral predator that Sam kept locked away came bursting out. His fingers tightened around the door handle letting his sharp claws dig into the metal as he let out a deep growl. He ripped the door from its frame, sending it flying down the hallway, and in a blur of fury, Sam rushed into the house, pinning the human monster to the floor. Before the man could scream for help, Sam bit into his throat, ripping out the voice box and making a quick meal of the piece of garbage who'd targeted young men and women. The human lured them to a dark alley, leaving their bodies to be found hours, sometimes days later. He'd left three of Sam's kind dead. He'd done unspeakable things to them before taking their lives, and Bast had ordered the man be eliminated.

Luckily the apartment complex was the home of people who were trying their best to avoid the law, which meant no one was going to bother helping their neighbor, but on the off chance someone did walk past, Sam made quick work of the rest of his mission. The others in his tribe wouldn't have to do the things he did. He cut up the leftovers to take back to the club. They wouldn't have to brave the streets and tarnish their souls by hunting down their next meal. That burden fell to Sam, Bast's hunter. The one person Bast had no problem sending out into the world to do the dirty work.

When the deed was done, Sam shoved the individual bags of meat into his backpack and slung it over his shoulder. Bast would flash freeze the meat to preserve it as soon as Sam brought it back, making it a fresh meal for the others. The color had left his eyes, and his teeth and hands had returned to normal. He was grateful for their quick transformations. Ghouls had a bad enough reputation thanks to the hordes of them who had no control over their urges.

Humans were convinced that ghouls devoured corpses and children, and it wasn't far from the truth for the uncivilized ones. But the small number of ghouls who'd adapted to the human world didn't need to eat an entire human to sustain their life. Strong enough emotions emitted some sustenance for the ghouls, allowing them to go longer between feedings. And these days humans gave off more than enough emotions. From hatred, fear, anger, love, lust. Most ghouls worked in fields that kept them in constant contact with highly emotional humans. Law enforcement, hospitals, bars. Now they only needed to consume meat on a very limited basis.

Even then, the ghouls like Sam had designated donors. Nursing homes and hospices were the perfect places to find a donor. Sick humans, ones with terminal diseases involving abnormal cell growth such as cancer, were usually offered a deal by the ghouls. The ghoul could eat the sickened growth, devour the diseased area, and offer the patient some relief. It would relieve their symptoms for months if not years in some cases. He wasn't sure why it worked that way, or why they couldn't completely cure the humans, but it was a chance for both creatures to sustain themselves for a little bit longer.

Heading down the stairs, Sam took the picture out of his back pocket. He needed something to pull his head from the past. The history of his people weighed heavy on his soul. The picture brought an instant wash of calm over him, and the woman made his mouth run dry. "Who are you?" Turning the photo over, he ran his thumb over the name written on the back again. Sam frowned. "Why is Rem so interested in you?" Shaking his head, he tucked the picture away and headed to the club to deliver his prey to Bast and call it a day.

"How long do you think we've been here?"

The small voice from the other side of the container drew Malia's attention. The little girl had asked the same question more times than she could count. Not that she could blame her. There was no way to track the passage of time, but Malia guessed it'd been at least a month in this particular container. They'd traveled by water for a long time, then by truck, and for the last part of their captivity, they'd sat in this place, wherever they were. Before being moved to this holding area, Malia had been kept for months alone in various other locations.

In the container, their captors would send someone in with food and water, but days would pass between visits. One by one they'd administer shots to the captives. Some people got the shot that would make them docile and complacent; others received a drug that caused the person to get progressively sicker. Malia received both injections. It didn't affect her. At most, it made her slightly relaxed, but it never incapacitated her. And while she wasn't in peak shape health-wise from the drugs, she wasn't suffering from the ill effects like the others in the container. She learned very quickly not to reveal that and played it up every time the guards came in to check on them.

The little girl asked again when no one answered, and this time one of the women snapped. "Shut the fuck up! Why do you keep asking the same fucking question? We don't know you stupid bi—"

Malia slammed the woman to the ground and pulled the girl behind her. "Leave her alone. She's scared, just like the rest of us." Turning to the girl, Malia knelt down. "We don't really know; it's probably been a month or longer."

"But why are they doing this? My mommy's been gone for a long time. They took her away, when are they bringing her back?'"

Malia's heart broke. They wouldn't be bringing the woman back; she had died in her sleep, along with several others, and Malia suspected several more would succumb with the next dose. She squeezed the girl tight. "She's not coming back. I'm sorry."

Another woman yelled, "Don't tell her that."

Malia snapped her head up. "She needs to know the truth; she has a right to know. We can't survive if we don't face reality."

"Is she dead?"

She turned back and held out her hands to the little girl. "I'm sorry, but yes. Your mom got sick from the shots they give us, and she didn't make it."

The child took Malia's hand and leaned against her as she wrapped her arms around Malia. "Am I going to die?"

She stroked the girl's hair. "I'm going to do everything I can to make sure that doesn't happen. What's your name, sweetie?"

"Ellie."

Standing up, Malia offered her hand again to Ellie. "I'm Malia, you stay close to me, and we'll stick this out together, okay?"

The girl's lip trembled, and she slipped her hand into Malia's as she settled back into the corner. The weight of the girl's head against her arm felt like the weight of the world. She had no idea what she was doing. She wasn't even sure how she was going to protect herself, let alone keep the girl safe, but now she at least had something else to focus on instead of trying to count the minutes and slowly driving herself insane. The guards had just left, and by all accounts, it would be a long time before they'd be back to collect anymore dead and administer their next dose of whatever they were pumping into them.

Sam leaned back against the bar of the nightclub and waited for Bast to finish doling out the food he'd brought back. When their colony's so-called leader came back out, he tossed a wad of money on the counter. "For your trouble."

Sam pushed the money aside as he always did. "It was no trouble. It's my job to provide for my people."

Bast slammed his fist down on the counter, and Sam regretted the words in an instant. "They aren't your people. They are mine; I am their leader, not you. You belong to me, boy. Don't forget your place."

Sam rolled his eyes. "Right, how could I forget."

Bast pointed a finger to the door. "You're free to go now, hunter. Your job here is done."

"So, eager to get rid of me, Bast?"

The older man glared. "You know, sometimes I think you get too big of a head on your shoulders thanks to that old man filling your brain with stories." He snorted and shook his head. "It's like he thinks you're the Black King or something."

Sam pushed off his stool and shoved his hands in his pockets, giving a little laugh. "Yeah, the Black King, wouldn't that be something." He didn't have to look back to know the color had drained from Bast's face, and the vein in his forehead was throbbing. Their leader always got like that when the subject of their tribe's destined leader came up. "No worries, right, Bast? I mean, you've seen me unleashed before, and you've never seen me with those black and red eyes. All in all, I'd say your position is safe. No supposed king is rising up to take your place."

He kept walking, never looking back, but he figured the reminder that Bast had never seen him with the tell-tale eyes of the last of the djinn's royal bloodline would be enough to soothe Bast's paranoia. The sign of the true king. As the cool wind hit his face, the red sheen started to coat his eyes as if his body wanted to claim what Sam wanted to deny. He kept his head down, walking down the street, reminding himself over and over that no one could ever find out about his eyes. Rem suspected, he always had, ever since he rescued Sam as a teenager. Maybe the man who'd saved him had actually caught a glimpse of his full transformation when he was a starving kid, but regardless, no amount of prodding from Rem would ever make him step up and take the crown. As he walked through the city, his mind drifted back to his childhood. Keeping his head down, he maneuvered through the streets while taking a mental stroll down memory lane.

He'd been a starving, insane creature, devouring corpses in cemeteries after his parents had been killed. He had no idea how to survive, and so he did what he could; he fed off the dead which drove him insane from the toxins in a rotting corpse. Then one night Rem appeared. He had a woman with him. Beautiful, with the voice of an angel. Her voice is what had calmed his mind, and Rem captured him.

Next thing Sam knew, he was waking up weeks later with a clear head, and Rem explained everything to him. His people, ghouls, were seen as monsters. But many centuries ago they had a different name, Djinn. Genies of great power with the ability to heal the sick and ease their pain. Over time they were captured, forced to be the slaves of powerful humans. Their numbers dwindled, and eventually, the world forgot about the djinn, and sadly they forgot about themselves. Driven mad by their hunger, they scavenged for the easiest available food. The dead. But once consumed, the decaying body became poison in the ghoul's system. It turned them insane. They lost their knowledge, their history, their identity. Then came the hunters. Now those hunters called themselves the Agency.

Lost in thought, Sam rounded the corner outside the club and bumped into someone. The man wore a dark suit, sunglasses, and had a .45 caliber pistol in a shoulder holster on his left side. Speak of the devil. The Agent grumbled a curse and shoved him. "Watch where you're going, asshole."

Sam muttered an apology and kept going. If the Agent knew what he was, Sam would've been killed on sight or held in one of the Agency's isolations cells to be tortured and made an example of. This new world of humans and paranormal creatures welcomed monsters, but not ghouls. They had no representation, no seat at either table. The Syndicate seemed to pretend they didn't exist, and the Agency was on a mission to exterminate them, or at least the ones like him who had a brain. The ones who didn't eat rotting corpses. They ate the living or at worse the recently killed, which kept them sane. It kept their thoughts clear, and it was one hundred percent illegal in the eyes of the Agency and the humans.

Sam was enemy number one on both of their lists. Pulling the picture out of his pocket again, he stared at the woman's face. Now, Rem wanted him to break into an Agency shipping yard and free this woman from a container. He thought back to Rem's words "I need it opened, and I need the items inside safely returned, but, there's one item in particular that I need secured." That meant that there were other humans in the container as well. He groaned. "All these years off the Agency's radar, and now I'm smack dab in the middle of this mess."

CHAPTER TWO

Malia tucked Ellie in behind her and pressed them both close into the corner of the shipping container as the doors opened and a tall female walked in. Malia couldn't be sure what sort of creatures her captors were, but she knew for certain they weren't human unlike all of the women in the container.

Days had passed, and she knew Ellie was starving, but food wasn't worth the price of being drugged. The girl had developed a cough and spiked a fever several times since Malia had taken her under her wing. Shielding Ellie with her body, Malia whispered, "Stay as quiet as possible. Maybe they won't see you."

"Everyone line up against the wall," their captor commanded.

The women all lined up, shoulder to shoulder, with an older woman standing next to Malia. Two males entered the container, and as usual, they went down the line. One counted the captives as he swabbed their arm with an alcohol pad, the next would inject them with whichever drug they were supposed to get, and lastly, the female would point out anyone who might be too sick or those who were already dead for the males to drag out. Every few days they would also bring in moldy bread and dirty water for the women to fight over. Malia sized them up. They carried nothing except their equipment. No food. If today wasn't a feeding day, then she had no clue how long Ellie and some of the others would last.

As the first male stepped in front of Malia, he looked her up and down. "Arm."

She turned slightly exposing her arm to him, and he cleaned the area. She shivered as his hand trailed up and his thumb caressed her neck. "Nice." He chuckled in her ear and licked up her cheek as his fang brushed against her flesh. Malia clenched her fist as he turned around. She could feel a cold sweat trickling down her neck; they were so close and yet every minute that ticked by was a chance for their captors to realize that someone was missing. He waved at his comrade. "This is the last one."

The person giving the shot injected the old woman and then took out another disposable syringe and stuck it in Malia's arm. "You get the cocktail again; you'll sell for a nice price. Boss says to keep you alive if possible. Enjoy your sleep, human." He gloated. She hissed at the sting and then moved to reposition herself to better shield Ellie. He turned to the female in charge and asked, "Any dead?"

"Not tonight." She walked up and down the line and finally pointed out the old woman, "Might as well take her, she probably won't last more than a few hours."

"I will; I'm not sick." The older woman protested.

"You won't; I can smell death on you."

"I'm not dying; I'm just old." She stepped forward and pointed a bony finger at the woman, "What do you want with an old woman like me anyway, you can't sell me on your black market."

"You," the female growled as she pushed the old woman back in line. "You are here strictly for research." She jutted her chin in Malia's direction and snarled. "Ones like her are here for a profit." Malia's stomach churned. She knew exactly what would happen to her, she knew what her fate was going to be, but that didn't mean she wanted to hear her captors say it out loud for the second time tonight. The female gave the other two a wave of her hand, dismissing them. On her way to the exit, she warned the old woman, "If you are worse tomorrow I'm sending you away, and you won't enjoy what I do to you."

Malia relaxed as the woman started to close their doors. She'd managed to hide Ellie, and for at least a little while longer the little girl might stand a chance of survival. The woman looked down at her clipboard and frowned. "Harris, you only counted twenty heads."

"Yeah, that's how many there were."

"According to our last head count, there should be twenty-one."

Malia's stomach dropped, and she reached back to grip Ellie's arm. The old woman looked up at Malia and pursed her lips together. Their captor stepped into the container again and counted, "Who is missing?" No one answered. She pulled out her gun and scanned the group. "Who's missing?"

Murmurs rose up from the captives, but still, no one answered. The woman adjusted her uniform, and Malia finally saw the glint of metal in the stream of moonlight that shown in from the open container doors. She was an Agent. They were being held by the Agency. The woman moved her gun and asked again, "Who is missing?"

When silence answered her, she fired a shot. One of the women fell to the floor. Her lifeless body marred by a single gunshot to the head. The woman Malia had defended Ellie against called out, "Ellie, the little girl, she's the one."

Malia cursed under her breath but the old woman was quick to action, she slapped the woman and warned. "You don't give up your own kind."

The Agent turned and leveled the gun at the old woman while flashing her bright white fangs. "Your own kind? What have your humans ever done for you? Is anyone even looking for you? For any of you? Your kind is weak and pathetic, and one day you will be nothing but a relic of the past. You will fade away because that is what happens when a new, stronger species rises to power."

The agent pulled the hammer back, and Ellie pushed out from behind Malia and yelled, "Don't shoot her."

Malia yanked her back to her side and braced her hands tight on the child's shoulders. The three agents turned, and the female agent narrowed her eyes. "Step forward."

Ellie took a step, but Malia tugged her back. "Leave her alone; she's just a child. Your drugs will kill her."

The woman pointed the gun at Malia. "I know that, but for scientific research, we need to know how many doses it will take. Now, let her go, or I will have to explain to my boss why I had to put a bullet in the head of the very pretty woman he's hoping to make a whole lot of money from selling."

"I don't care; I'd rather die," Malia shot back.

Before she could think, the woman leveled the gun at Ellie. "And how about her, would you want to have her brains splattered all over you?"

Malia drew in a breath and Ellie stepped out into the open. Pulling up her sleeve, she turned her head to the side, her little chin jutting out defiantly. "Don't hurt her."

"Brave one, aren't you," the woman taunted as the men administered the drug, and all three of them left without another word.

Malia scooped Ellie up and held her tight. The entire group was fading fast. Adrenaline only kept them coherent for a short time and now, one by one they were all slipping under the effects of the drug. One of the women started to seize, and the old woman hit the floor with a thud. If she could help them, she would, but she had no explanation why she wasn't affected. As Ellie started to go limp in her arms, she buckled into a heap on the floor, rocking the little girl as her breathing grew softer and her heartbeat slowed.

She drifted off to sleep singing songs to Ellie. The little girl hadn't once opened her eyes, but Malia could feel the rise and fall of her chest, so she knew Ellie was still alive. None of the others had stirred, and if history were any indication, it would be hours before they'd wake, and some of them wouldn't wake at all.

Reaching over, she felt for the older woman in the dark. When she found her body, Malia scooted her and Ellie closer and ran her hand up to the woman's neck. She closed her eyes. No pulse. The body was cold and stiff. "Shit," she whispered.

Setting Ellie down carefully, she made her way one by one to each of the bodies. They were either not breathing or just barely. "Why me?" she asked out loud as if someone would give her an answer. Nothing happened. Of the twenty-one remaining humans, seven had already died, six were barely holding on, and the rest were like Ellie. Deeply sedated and unable to move.

Malia came back to her corner and sat back down, bringing Ellie back into her lap. She stroked her hair, humming softly to her like she imagined someone would have done for her if she'd had someone to look out for her after her father had passed away.

As the time passed, Malia faded in and out of sleep, and eventually, the survivors started to rouse. They were groggy at first, but soon they'd be almost back to normal. One of the side effects for some was the loss of speech, and the man who'd yelled at Ellie found himself stricken mute. He frantically gripped his throat as if trying to squeeze sound out of it. Malia looked away and turned her attention to Ellie.

A banging noise rose up, something metal hitting against their shipping container. The noise was terrible. It echoed off the walls, and the sound seemed to get louder with every hit. Everyone who was awake covered their ears. Ellie woke up and slapped her hands over her ears. "What's that noise?"

"I don't know," Malia shouted over the banging. "Just hold still."

One final hit and the doors swung open. Moonlight poured in, and a man stood holding both doors open. Head bowed, he seemed to be breathing heavy, and Malia caught sight of blond hair peeking out from the hood covering his head. "Everyone ready?" he asked.

The humans in the container all stared and blinked. Most of them were still fighting off the effects of the drugs. Malia stood up, picking up Ellie with her and moved to the doors. "Ready for what?"

He looked up, meeting her gaze, and Malia sucked in a breath. His blue eyes were locked on her as if he was there just for her. "To escape. This is a rescue."

Not meaning to sound cynical, but one man against the agency seemed far-fetched. "You and what army?"

"No army, just me. Do you want to get out of here or what?"

"Yes." Looking back at the other people she sighed. "They can't move fast on their own; they need help."

He motioned her for her to step out, and as soon as she did, he pointed to a boat tied to the dock. "Let's get you out of here first and then I'll get the others."

She paused and held Ellie tight. "I'll help get the others; they're in bad shape."

The man didn't seem to like the idea, but she'd already gone back in the container and helped one of the women to her feet. She slung the woman's arm over her shoulder, still balancing Ellie on her hip, and slowly helped her out onto the dock and into the boat. In the time it took her to help one person, the man had already moved three others, and he insisted that she stay on the boat this time while he helped the last two captives.

While he ran to get the women out, Malia stood up on the boat and looked around. The bright moonlight lit up the shipping yard, and Malia saw the mess the man had left in his wake trying to free them. At least a dozen armed guards were knocked out or dead, she couldn't tell from the boat, but spotting some puddles of what could be blood around some of the bodies made her think they wouldn't be waking up from their injuries. Not that she felt any sympathy for them. For all she cared, they could rot in hell for the part they played in holding them all prisoner.

The man came back out with the last of the women and called out, "Start the engine."

She blinked and spun around looking at the dashboard. "I don't know how."

The sound of sirens echoed down the empty street, and a cold panic hit Malia. One of the women pointed to the dash, and she quickly followed her directions. The engine turned over as soon as the mystery man jumped on board. He placed the last two people on the floor and took control of the boat.

Malia sat silently watching the digital clock on the dash and listening to Ellie's exuberant squeals every time the boat crashed into a wave. "Who are you?" she finally asked.

"A concerned citizen," was his response.

She shrugged it off. Maybe he was some sort of vigilante and wanted to keep his identity a secret. Clearing her throat, she shouted over the sound of the engine. "What's the date?"

He looked back at the other passengers, all of them had fallen back asleep. "It's July."

Malia gasped. "Four months? I've been in that damn metal prison for four months?" Anger bubbled up inside of her. She had never felt so much fury and rage before. The Agency had stolen four months of her life.

Ellie turned and stroked her cheek. "It's okay; we're safe now. He saved us."

Malia narrowed her eyes at the man. He had saved them, but so far had offered no information except for the month. He could be leading them into a trap, or worse, to the auction block. Ellie doubled over, her cough stealing her breath away just as she was about to say something. Malia winced, wishing she could take the pain away as tears streaked Ellie's face. Nothing would help, but she still rubbed circles over the girl's back and gave light pats to help when it sounded like phlegm was lodged in Ellie's throat.

"What's wrong with her?"

"The drug they've been giving us. It makes them all sick."

"Them, but not you?" He turned again to look at her, and she got the distinct impression he was searching for something.

"It does something to me, but I haven't gotten as sick as everyone else." When he opened his mouth, she held up her hand to stop him. "I don't know why, so don't bother asking."

Slowing the boat, he opened a small door and motioned for her to follow. "We've got a few hours to go, why don't you take your daughter down there and get her out of the cold night air."

The last thing she wanted was to be trapped inside a small space again, but the chill from the breeze on the water couldn't be good for Ellie's cough. With a nod, she picked her up and headed below deck. She paused at the door and offered, "She's not my daughter. Her mom died in that box."

"Well, you're all she has now, and it seems like you're doing a good job."

"Are you ever going to tell me your name?"

His smile sent a chill down her spine, and her mouth went dry. "Rest for now; we'll talk when we get you all settled." She didn't get a chance to ask anything else as he shooed her down the small stairs and called out as the door shut, "I'll let you know when we make land."

When the boat docked, sunlight was just starting to brighten the horizon. The other women were still asleep, and their savior stood quietly at the steering wheel. She cleared her throat. "Where are we? And are you ever going to explain what's going on?"

He turned, flashing that devastating smile that sent her head spinning. "We came down the coastline. I figured putting some mileage between the Agency and us would buy us some time to sort everything out."

"But where are we supposed to go?"

"Home, presumably. Where are you from?"

She blinked and tried to pinpoint a place of reference and shook her head. "I don't really have a home. I was staying in Montreal, I had a temp job there, but it wasn't home, and I certainly don't want to go back to where I was taken."

He nodded. "Makes sense. Well, we have to meet up with the man who orchestrated all this. Knowing him, he'll have something planned. He always does."

"So, you have a boss? Who do you work for?"

The man laughed. "Rem's not my boss; he's my friend."

"You risk your life for a friend?"

He stepped onto the dock and looked down at her. "I risked my life because it was the right thing to do and I had the means to do it."

"I'm glad it was someone like you and not some werewolf or vampire."

His brow arched. "Not a fan of the paranormal, are you?"

"Not at all. Especially now that I know it was the Agency who abducted us. They were supposed to be the ones protecting us from those creatures. I think I'd like to stick to my own kind for a while." She let out a low whistle and handed Ellie to him. "I wish more guys were like you. Hell, I wish more humans, in general, were helpful. Most of us just turn away and don't help."

Something passed behind his eyes, but he offered a hand to help her off the boat. "I'm sure anyone would have helped if they could. I'm Sam by the way."

She smiled. "Malia. Nice to meet you."

Sam leaned against the back wall of the farmhouse where he'd stopped with the group. The boat was long gone, and he'd backtracked the rescued women north to a small farm a couple of states away from the rescue site. The best part about the East Coast was how quickly you could jump state lines when you were in a hurry. His phone rang, and Sam answered it before the first ring had time to finish. "Rem? Man, I've been trying to reach you."

"I know, sorry. I was in a meeting."

The background noise of a club came through the phone, and Sam shook his head. "Yeah, that sounds like a meeting. What do you want me to do with these humans? They are scared, and some of them aren't getting any better. They're all drifters, no real home to speak of, no family, and not surprisingly they don't want to return to their old lives."

"They don't?"

Rem sounded genuinely confused as if he hadn't expected that, and Sam pinched the bridge of his nose. "Rem, they're scared to go because they think they might get abducted again. That girl, the one in the picture, she was in Montreal, but she doesn't want to go back there. All the others feel the same."

There was no response on the other end of the line, and two seconds later the call dropped. Sam looked at his phone and cursed before shoving it in his pocket. "Don't be so disappointed, son." Rem's voice came from the dark corner of the house, and Sam laughed.

"Hate it when you do that."

"I know, which is why I only do it if it's absolutely necessary." Rem came out from the darkness and patted Sam's shoulders. "Take me to meet them."

Sam led Rem out into the large living room where seven of the survivors were sitting. Some had drifted back off to sleep; others just sat staring off at nothing. Rem leaned over and asked. "Weren't there more?"

Sam's shoulders slumped. "Malia is upstairs laying down with a little girl. The others didn't make it."

"Why? What is going on with them? I thought the Agency was holding them to sell as slaves."

Sam covered his mouth as he whispered. "They were keeping some of them to sell. Others they were keeping as experiments, to see how some new drug they've been pushing affects people of different ages."

"And Malia? Is she sick?"

Sam shook his head. "She seems fine, a bit tired, but not as bad as the others. The little girl though, she's not doing so good."

Rem stepped forward and spoke to the group. "Excuse me?"

The women opened their eyes, even the ones in a deep sleep suddenly sat up paying full attention to Rem. Sam left the room and headed for the stairs but could hear Rem talking to them, finding out everything he could about them, and like most people, they were opening up their life stories to the man. He couldn't help but smile, memories of his first conversation with Rem played in his head. The man had a soothing aura around him; it made you feel safe and comfortable. As he reached the landing, he scented the air, catching Malia's scent down the hallway in the master bedroom.

He approached slowly and knocked. "Malia, can I come in?"

"Yeah, it's open."

Opening the door, he stepped inside to find the girl laying on the bed and Malia sitting in a chair next to her with a bucket at her feet and a pile of wet clothes tossed aside. "How's she doing?"

"Her fever breaks for a few moments, but then the vomiting and fever come back. I don't know what to do."

Sam moved to the bed, stepping between Malia and the bed and laid his hand on Ellie's forehead. "Damn."

"Yeah, she's burning up."

It wasn't just the fever. He could feel her life force draining, not fast, but like the slow trickle of a leaky faucet. Even worse, he couldn't taste the sickness. If he could taste it, he could find it, maybe find a way to abate the symptoms or cure her completely, but there was nothing there as if she wasn't sick at all. But she was, he could feel it and see it. But his power wouldn't do him any good here. In cases where the dying person isn't sick, doesn't have a disease or illness, a ghoul's power was useless except for one option, but turning the child wasn't a choice he could make.

Malia had made it clear that she thought he was human, and after what the paranormal agency just did to them, he was going to do everything he could to keep her from learning the truth. Drawing away his hand and stepping back, Sam shoved his hands in his pockets. "My friend is here; I think he'll want to speak with you when he finishes up downstairs."

A panic entered her eyes, and Malia spun in the chair. "Why? What's he doing to them? Are they safe? Or--"

Sam's brows creased. "Or what?"

"Is this real? Did you really save us or is this some big elaborate hoax and you're really going to sell us just like the Agency was going to do?"

Sam felt his mouth fall open. He took a step back again and held up his hands. "I have no intention of selling you or anyone else. It really was a rescue."

"But why? Why would you and this friend of yours give a shit about any of us? Why save us? We are nothing."

Sam opened his mouth to speak, but Rem cut him off. "You are not nothing, Malia." Even knowing that Rem was a friend, hell, the closest thing Sam had to a father, he still moved on instinct to step between Malia and Rem. There was something in Rem's eyes that lit up, not with anger but with delight at the gesture. Inwardly Sam reminded himself that he could probably live two hundred years and still not figure that man out.

Malia, on the other hand, made a grunting noise and placed her hand on Sam's arm and softly pushed him aside as she stood up. "Who are you?"

"My name is Rem; we are family."

Sam's breath caught in his chest. She was Rem's family? No wonder he'd sent Sam. A second thought went rushing through his mind. Why would he send Sam? For that matter, what the hell was Rem's family doing in that shipping container? After finally finding the voice to speak, he motioned for the door. "I'm going to leave you two alone to talk." One last protective instinct rose up, and he met Malia's gaze. "Is that alright?"

She glanced from Sam to Rem and back to Sam again. "You trust him, right?" When he nodded, she offered a small smile. "I'll be fine."

Malia stood to watch as Sam quickly made his exit. A million and one questions were on the tip of her tongue, but she couldn't form a single word.

The dapper man with long silver hair and swirling eyes held her gaze. There was something vaguely familiar about him, but she knew she'd never met him before. She would remember meeting someone with those eyes. He wore a tailored suit, black with a sky-blue shirt and a matching pocket square. He smiled, and it practically lit up the room. And when he spoke, it sounded akin to the heavens opening up and raining down calm over her. "Hello, Malia."

"Hi," she responded timidly.

"How are you?"

He was speaking with all the patience of a parent coaxing a scared child. She frowned. "How are we related?"

His eyes lit up, and he chuckled. "Straight to the point, I see, the apple doesn't fall far from the tree."

"Who's tree?"

"The gods'." She expected another chuckle or for his eyes to dance with delight again, but instead he was completely serious.

"Excuse me?"

He shrugged off the question and asked one of his own. "What is your last name? Tell me about your parents?

"My last name is Rhea." As soon as the words left her mouth, the man sucked in a breath. Shaking her head, she continued, "My dad's name was Vasilios, my mother's name was Helen."

"Vasilios? Of royal blood," the man murmured. "You're Greek, yes?"

"Partly. My dad was a very proud Greek, but he always told me that our strong blood comes from Rome. Apparently, his family was from there. My mom was French but grew up in the states, so I didn't get much information from her side of the family."

"And where are your parents, now?"

Malia flinched. "My mom died when I was three. My father passed away ten years later."

He moved to the end of the bed and sat down, glancing over at Ellie's sleeping form and placing a hand on her leg which seemed to stop her tremors. He brought his attention back to her and asked, "You were alone since you were thirteen? No other family?"

She shook her head. There was no reason she should be sharing this information with a total stranger, but something inside her compelled her to be truthful. "After that, it was just me. Are you going to tell me how you think we are related?"

"I will, but first, where are your belongings? You'd told Sam you didn't have a home, but you'd worked in Montreal. Did you have anything sentimental in your belongings?"

"Yes, actually, but I'll never get it back." She crossed her arms over her chest. "The people that kidnapped me, they ransacked my apartment until they found a necklace that my father had given to my mother. He said it was his birthright, his only inheritance. After she died, he gave it to me."

"The Agency took it?"

She nodded. He motioned for her to sit, and when she did, he continued, "Can you describe it to me?"

"Yeah, it was a metal medallion of the Roman Empire symbol, but flipped the wrong way."

"And?" he pressed.

"And surrounded by a wreath. Half oak leaves—"

"And the other half an olive branch," he finished for her.

Malia blinked. "How did you know that?"

He pulled an exact copy of her father's necklace out of his shirt. "I am that Roman blood that flows through your veins."

"I don't understand."

"This is my symbol, Malia." He looked deep into her eyes. "What I'm going to tell you is for your ears only."

"Sam?"

He shook his head. "Sam doesn't know this, although he is a bright man, he might suspect."

She held her breath and darted her eyes to the door. "Don't you trust Sam?"

"I trust Sam with everything and anything that is precious to me. Sam is always loyal, but I've tried to protect him from certain truths. I've tried to shelter him, and I'm afraid in doing so I've done him a disservice. In time Sam will find out, but for now, this is between you and me."

"Okay."

"That symbol that your father called his birthright is my symbol. The symbol I took almost three thousand years ago after my brother, Romulus, murdered me and claimed control of our city, the city we had designed and planned for together. Romulus became the founder of Rome. I was left to die, but my brother didn't count on my survival. I rose to find power of my own, to form a society, and I kept it a secret for many, many centuries."

"You had children?"

"Yes, sowing your oats was sort of the thing to do for demigods." His gaze moved to Ellie and then back to Malia. "I assume my brother did as well. But you, if your father had my medallion, then you are of my bloodline. My great, great times god knows how many great granddaughter."

"Your name isn't Rem..." She trailed off and stared at the metal dangling from the chain. "You're Remus Silvia."

"Long dead demigod and founder of a new resistance," he chuckled. "You know your history."

"What does your resistance do?"

"They fight against Romulus; they try to stop the spread of his power and corruption."

Malia looked over at Ellie sleeping peacefully. "Am I a demigod? Because I don't feel anything."

"I think it's so diluted that you don't have any accessible power, but I can still hear the call of your blood. Power still runs through you. Tell me, do you get sick often?"

She shook her head. "I've never had a cold in my life." He smiled and she wanted to return it with one of her own but she looked at Ellie again, and her heart dropped. "The drug didn't affect me like it did the others either."

"You're immune?"

Malia bit her lip. "I don't think so, it had an effect, just not that bad. I didn't get sick from it, it didn't knock me out, or give me seizures, but I could feel it. It made me weak, tired, but I could still function."

Remus stood up and tucked the medallion back in his shirt. "The agency targeted you for a reason; Romulus knew who you were which is why they were looking for your necklace. It's also why they were going to sell you or kill you. It was personal." He offered a kind smile and headed toward the door. "We will talk more soon, but I need you to help Sam and stay with him so that I can know he's protecting you. We'll find places for everyone else and get them somewhere safe."

Malia jumped to her feet. "I'm not leaving Ellie. She goes with me."

"Malia, the child is—"

"Sick, yes I know. If you're such a demigod, then heal her." He didn't answer, and she glared. "She stays with me; her mother died in that container, and I made a promise. Where I go, she goes."

"Very well, but eventually someone might take notice; we will need to come up with a cover for you two." Opening the door, he called down the hallway, "Sam, you can come back in." Remus looked over his shoulder at her and smiled one last time. "Remember what I said. Our little secret and you stay with Sam. He will keep both of you safe."

CHAPTER THREE

Two days later she'd found herself standing outside of a corner shop. Ellie was having a moment of clarity and stood next to her, hand firmly grasping Malia's. Both of them looked at the sign and then at Sam. "Better Off Read - Books and Periodicals. Why are we at a bookstore?"

"We're home," Sam said as he unlocked the door. "Well, not we, but you and Ellie are home." Once they got inside and he locked the shop behind them, he led them to a door in the back. The door hid a flight of stairs and at the top, another door. Turning the handle, Sam opened the door wide enough for them to pass and closed it behind them. "This is my apartment. Sorry, it's not much to look at, but it'll be a roof over your heads and a good place to hide."

Malia walked around the open living room; the entire wall was windows looking out on the street below. "It's beautiful, but where will you stay?"

"In the store." Before she could protest, he waved his hand. "There's an unused room down there; I can convert it into a bedroom."

"No, you shouldn't have to rearrange your life for us. I mean, couldn't Rem find us a hotel or something?"

Sam shook his head. "It's not a problem. I don't mind, and I'd rather have you close just in case." His eyes averted to settle on Ellie already curled up on the couch and starting to close her eyes. He lowered his voice, "In case something happens."

She sighed and moved through the house; the living room at the front of the apartment butted up with the bar counter of the kitchen, which then led to the two bedrooms and a shared bathroom. It was small, neat, and comfy. When she came back to the kitchen, she leaned against the counter and cocked her head to the side to size him up. "Why are you doing all this for us, Sam?"

He took a step closer and a warm buzz centered in her gut. "Maybe I'm just a good guy."

She shook her head. "I saw what happened to the men on the docks that night; I don't think you're a good guy."

His smile faded just a bit as he held her gaze. "Do you think I'm a bad guy?"

She smiled, "No, just not necessarily good."

He pressed his hand over his chest and laughed. "That's a cruel thing to say."

Malia's grin grew larger. "Did I hurt your feelings?"

"You did. It might take me some time to heal."

His playfulness had been putting her at ease over the past few days. When she would otherwise find herself dwelling on the ordeal, he kept her grounded in the here and now, and she couldn't have asked for a better distraction. He stepped closer to her, and she eyed him. Something sparked to life every time he got near. It made her hands itch to touch him. It was more than the dashing smile or the deep voice that sent a shiver down her spine. It was something under the surface, and it ate at her.

She licked her lips, letting her eyes travel down his body. Sam took another step forward, and she gripped the edge of the counter. He was so close now she could smell his scent. It wasn't cologne, but it was intoxicating. "Sam," her words came out more breathily than she'd intended, and he took another step.

His body pressed against her, sending her head spinning. Placing her palm on his chest, she held it there just feeling the rhythm of his heartbeat and breathing. It was reassuring to find a man who wasn't a vampire or werewolf, who was just a good man and admittedly had the looks that could rival any vamp she'd seen. His hand covered hers, and her breath hitched.

A deep rumble came from him, and she looked up to see him staring at her. "Sam, I—"

She didn't even know what she wanted to say; she wanted to say everything and nothing at the same time. She'd been denied human interaction for so long in captivity that she desperately wanted to devour every sensation of touch and taste and sound. And she wanted to have that all with him. His head dipped, and Malia held her breath, counting the seconds, waiting for sweet contact, but it didn't come. She hadn't even realized she'd closed her eyes until she heard him. "Malia?"

She opened her eyes. He was less than an inch from her face. His lips so close that his breath fanned over hers, making her legs shake. "Yes?"

His hand braced on the counter next to hers, and she could feel the tension rolling off of him. He swallowed several times. "I need to go."

"Why?"

"Because you are... You need rest, and you'll both need some food soon."

She shook her head. "Don't go." He had started to say something else, and for the life of her, she wanted to know what he'd been about to say.

"I can't stay."

Her mind went blank at that moment. All the stress, all the fear, all the anxiety over the entire course of her captivity shattered, and she leaned forward. Her lips pressed against his, and to her shock, Sam stayed completely still. He didn't reciprocate, he didn't return the kiss, and as she snapped back into reality, tears welled up in her eyes. She didn't let them fall; instead, she leaned back and covered her raw emotions with a laugh. "Sorry, I just had to get that out of the way."

He looked utterly confused. Rubbing the back of his neck, he slid one foot back. "Get it out of the way?"

"Yeah," she coughed, still trying to choke down the tears threatening to escape. "You know, pent-up stress. I figure it was better than screaming or breaking stuff. Won't happen a—"

His hand caught the back of her neck, pulling her to him, and he captured her mouth with his. She moaned against his lips, letting his tongue stroke hers. Heat coursed through her, and the hairs on her arm stood on end as his hand tangled in her hair.

It ended as quickly as it began and Malia felt something building up inside her. More. She needed more. Sam stepped back and smiled. "Did that help?"

She nodded but inside she was screaming. It hadn't helped, it had made it worse. She needed to release all the pent-up emotions before she exploded, and yet Sam being what she could only consider noble in his own way, had just made the whole damn thing worse. He took several steps back, putting even more distance between them, making her ache even more and gestured to the door. "Lock up after I leave; I'll make sure the alarm is set, but just to be safe."

"You're really going?"

"I've got to. Ellie will be awake soon; and she'll need food. Besides..." He shook his head. "Never mind."

"No, tell me. Besides, what?"

"Malia, I—"

"Yes?" she prodded.

"I want you." He looked up at the ceiling and cursed. "God damn, woman, you have to know what just being near you does to me." He looked back down and shoved his hands into his pockets. "You need space, and I need fresh air."

"Because you want me?"

"Yes."

Her brow quirked at the absurdity of his thinking. He had to go because he wanted her? That didn't even make sense. "And?"

"You just survived a huge trauma; it's not really the time for a hookup."

"Maybe that's exactly what I need."

He closed the space between them again and cupped her cheek. Malia leaned into his hand and looked up at him. Sam stroked her cheek and shook his head. "No, it's not. Sex will just cloud everything more. Trust me; you need time to heal. I'm going to give you that time."

"I'm not hurt, Sam." She tried to coax him, running her hand down his chest.

"Not physically." His other hand tapped her head and then slid down her neck to splay out over her chest. "Not physically, but you did go through some bad shit. I won't hurt you more by taking advantage of that."

"But I want—"

He pressed a kiss to her forehead, silencing her, and whispered, "I'll bring you guys some food. Get some rest, beautiful."

She wanted to yell at him, to rally against him for insinuating that she was somehow mentally or emotionally broken because of what happened, but his words sunk in leaving her speechless. He'd called her beautiful, and he wasn't having sex with her because he didn't want to hurt her.

As he turned the door handle, she swallowed the lump in her throat and offered up a small smile. "Thank you, Sam."

He closed the door behind him, and Malia's tears came as soon as the door shut. Everything inside of her shattered, and she covered her face, sobbing so deeply she couldn't catch her breath. Sliding down the cupboard, she sat huddled on the kitchen floor crying until her entire world went black and darkness pulled her under.

Sam leaned against the door and took a deep breath. Malia's sobbing left an ache in his chest. His hands shook as he slid down the door and sat on the stairs. He wanted to go back in there and do anything to make her stop crying. "If I go in there, I will give in." As her cries started to lessen, he pulled out his phone and quietly made his way downstairs while dialing a number. As soon as the woman on the other end picked up, he cleared his throat. "It's Sam. I need help."

"What is it? You need a session?" the woman taunted.

He swallowed and punched in the security code before leaving the building. "Not for me, someone else."

"A..." There was a pause, "family member?"

"No, she's human."

"Oh." Her tone turned into a joy that made his stomach churn. Feeding off of emotions was better than eating people, but he didn't like the idea of someone feeding on Malia, not for this, although no harm came to the people they fed on.

"I'm not offering her up as a meal."

"You know we don't hurt them."

"She needs help, and you're the only one I can turn to."

"If you are suddenly so offended by what we do, then why call me at all?"

"Mary, you're the only one I can turn to. She needs help, and I can't give it to her. I'll fuck it all up and damage her more."

There was a sigh from the other end of the phone. "Tell me what I'm working with."

"She was abducted along with several others for some sort of slave trade. She was locked up for four months in a shipping container. She's been through some bad shit. She needs a safe place to talk about it and get it all out."

"I can see her—" A knock came through the phone, "Someone's here, hold on, but I think I can get her in next week."

"No, it needs to be sooner," he protested, but from the muffled voices he could hear through the phone, she wasn't listening to him.

Moments later she picked the phone back up and coughed. "Never mind, I can see her tonight, if that works. I'll come by. Where is she staying?"

The hairs on Sam's next stood on end. "Um, yeah, sure. She's on the lower east side. It's a small apartment she shares with her boyfriend. I'll text you the address. Thanks for the help."

She waited several seconds and then cleared her throat again. "I'm sorry, Abraham." A cold sweat broke out on his forehead. What the hell was going on? "I just want you to be prepared; sometimes in cases like this the person is just too damaged from the events, and there is no getting better, but I will work with her. Will you be joining us tonight?"

"No, I—"

Her voice rose, and Sam's grip on the phone tightened. "Oh, good. It'll be nice to catch up. You've been away so long. Hopefully we can grab dinner afterward. See you tonight."

The line went dead, and Sam stared at the call screen. "What the fuck?" Mary, one of his own, had just betrayed him, set Malia up to probably be recaptured or worse. His longtime friend had given him a heads up, she'd said enough to let him know something was wrong, but the betrayal still cut deep. He flipped through his phone, and as promised, quickly texted her the address of the man he'd harvested for the colony days earlier. The Agency could have fun finding that mess. After the text sent, he pulled up Rem's number and hit send. Rem answered before the phone even rang. "Hey, Rem, I need a favor."

"What is it?"

"Malia needs some help." Sam stopped at a nearby alleyway and stepped into its shadows. "She needs someone to help her process everything that happened. I called one of my people, but I'm pretty sure the Agency showed up and—"

"And what?"

"I think she betrayed me and made some sort of deal with them, but I have no idea how they would have known to go to her? I mean she's completely off their radar."

Rem didn't miss a beat as he broke it all down in quick secession. "They have psychics, telepaths, even mediums who converse with the spirits. They'll use anyone and everyone they can to gather information. At this moment, I want you to trust only me and people I directly put you in contact with. If they went to your friend, they still don't have a beat on Malia or you, my guess is they got a little scrap of info about Malia seeing this woman and they are hoping they can get the jump on you two. I've got someone for her to talk to. She'll meet you two at the Starlight Lounge in," there was a pause, and Rem muttered to himself, "Um, in two hours. Bring the girl too; we can have my doctor look her over while Malia has a session with Reagan."

Sam scratched his chin. "And you trust this Reagan person?"

"Absolutely, as much as I trust you, son. Don't worry; I've got some talented people in my pocket, I'll make sure someone wards your shop and apartment, and we'll cloak Ellie and Malia from any more psychic or otherworldly tracking."

That was all the reassurances Sam needed, plus knowing that Rem and Malia were related helped put him at ease that no harm would come to her or Ellie while at the Starlight. He stepped out onto the street and headed for a small family grocer on the corner. Gathering up some soup, bread, and other staples he headed back and prayed that by the time he got inside that Malia would have fallen asleep and he wouldn't have to face rejecting her once more.

The dim lights of the Starlight Lounge greeted them along with a lot of sidelong stares at Sam and Malia with Ellie in tow. One of the waitresses approached and held out her hand. "I'm Starla, welcome to my place." After Malia and Sam shook her hand, she bent down to Ellie and smiled. "You must be Ellie. Would you like to come with me and play some games while your mom visits with Ms. Reagan?"

Malia's eyes went wide. "Oh, I'm not—"

Ellie squeezed Malia's hand and shook her head. "It's alright."

Starla looked back and forth between them. "I'm sorry, I just assumed. I apologize."

Ellie leaned against Malia but raised her chin up and met Starla's gaze. "It's alright, my mommy died, so I guess that makes Malia my mom now."

Malia's hand shook. She wanted to protect Ellie from the harsh realities of the world, but Ellie had already faced those harsh realities. Sam gave a reassuring squeeze to her shoulder as she bent down to talk to Ellie. "This shouldn't take too long, are you sure you'll be alright?"

Ellie smiled. "Don't worry." A string of coughs racked the little girl for several seconds, but as soon as they passed, she smiled again. "I'll be fine, and Sam can come play with us too."

Sam laughed. "I'll be there as soon as possible."

Ellie gave a stern nod and grabbed Starla's hand, taking the beautiful woman back by the action, and headed towards the door near the back of the stage. The little girl rattled on, practically dragging the woman behind her. "I have a feeling you've got games back here. I've been in clubs like this before; you keep them in the ladies dressing rooms right."

They disappeared behind the door before Malia could hear Starla's response. She wrinkled up her nose. "How would the kid know that?"

Sam shrugged and walked to a door near the bar marked Private. "Maybe her mom worked at a place like this. Come on, let's go meet this person."

He opened the door, and Malia stepped in to find a young woman sitting behind the desk. She had long brown hair and blue eyes, and as she stood up, Malia focused on the slight bump protruding from her belly. Quickly she snapped her eyes up to greet the woman, "You must be Reagan?"

"Yes, Rem—" she paused and cleared her throat, "Rem has told me a little bit about the situation, but for this first session I'd like to hear everything straight from you." Reagan turned to Sam and motioned for the door. "We'll be fine in here, Starla has the best security, you don't have to worry. Rem is outside waiting for you at table six."

Malia watched as her protector left and shut the door. Turning slowly back to face the woman at the desk Malia crossed her arms. "So, you're pregnant?"

Reagan smiled and waggled her finger. "Oh, no. You don't get to deflect." Malia crossed her arms and Reagan continued. "You have some serious issues to work out, and like it or not, we are going to work through them."

"There's nothing wrong with me. Why does everyone keep saying that?"

Reagan shrugged. "Who else has mentioned it?"

"Sam." She flopped down in the chair and drummed her fingers on the leather armrests. "He seems to think I need this, so I'm doing this for him, but

I'm telling you I'm fine. I just needed some release, I had some pent-up energy, and I wanted to let it loose."

"And what did you try to do to let it loose?"

"I—" Malia shifted her gaze to a speck of glitter on the floor, her drumming fingers slowed, and it took several swallows to get her voice to actually work. "I tried throwing myself at Sam, who of course, rejected me."

"Why do you say it like that?" Reagan pried.

"Say what?"

"That he 'of course' rejected you."

"Because, I mean, it's obvious, right?" She motioned towards the door. "You saw him; he's amazing and gorgeous..."

"And?"

Malia concentrated on the glitter again. "Here I am, some chick he rescued only because it was a job, who he's now stuck with living at his house, with a kid, ruining his life, and to top it off she's the victim of human trafficking where they were going to sell her as a sex slave. Of course, he wouldn't want any part of me. Probably thinks I've been passed around and used by the people who abducted me. Probably doesn't want that stain on his score sheet. Probably pities me, which is why he's doing this, bringing me here to see you."

"Malia, that's a whole lot of assumptions, and I'm sure Sam doesn't think that way at all about you, but you know what," Reagan leaned back in her chair and rested her hands on her belly, "it's pretty telling that that is how you see it."

Malia looked away as soon as her gaze met Reagan's. She focused on the floor again. "I'm broken, aren't I?"

"The type of trauma you've endured would mess-up anyone, Malia; you need to work through all of this. People tend to try to repress what happened; we try to substitute feelings with things like sex, reckless behavior, and drugs to keep from feeling the pain of working through our feelings. I believe that is what you tried to do with Sam. You wanted to use him to fill the void that your pain and fear has left, and if you had done that, you would have felt worse afterward because it never helps. What helps is working through it. Sam cares enough for you that he walked away and he brought you here. I don't think he feels like you are ruining his life. You have some good support from that man, even if he is a stranger. Sometimes, it's the people we barely know that care the most about us."

"Will I get better?"

"Yes, without a doubt."

Malia lifted her chin and set her jaw. "Okay, let's do this."

CHAPTER FOUR

"It's been almost a month, Sam," Malia called out from the kitchen.

He rolled his head back. "Hmm?"

She watched him from her vantage point and shook her head. After sitting with Ellie over half the night, they were both exhausted, but it'd been their life for the past several weeks. "Why isn't she getting better? The drugs are long gone from her system."

"I don't know. I've researched everything I could find on long-lasting drug effects." He'd made his way into the kitchen and did a quick peek down the hallway. "She's sleeping now."

Malia wiped her hands on a towel. "Finally. I don't know how to help her." As she scooped him up a plate of spaghetti, she asked, "Any word from Rem? I mean, he's got to have a way to help, right?"

Sam shook his head. "He hasn't found anything; last I heard he was out of town looking for any information about what ingredients the Agency is using to make their drug." After taking a bite and then setting the plate aside, Sam took a step closer. "She's not getting better. The time between fevers and pain is getting shorter and shorter—"

Malia placed her hand on his chest, and she felt him stiffen. Their physical contact had been extremely limited since she'd started seeing Reagan multiple times a week, but touching him made her feel a bit more grounded, and she wasn't feeling the same break-neck need for release like she had before. Now it was more just comfort and familiarity to reach out and feel him near her. "We need to find out. Find someone in the Agency and make them talk."

"We're not hired thugs, Malia. Do you know how to interrogate someone? Especially someone trained on how to survive an interrogation? We would come up with nothing, or worst-case scenario, they'd capture us and then Ellie would be all alone. You can't leave her without a mother." He reached out and cupped her cheek, "And if I go, it'd leave both of you without protection."

"But we need to—"

"I didn't say I was giving up. I've made some contacts with people that Rem trusts, but I can't go rushing in and tear the place apart looking for god knows what."

She bit her lip and nodded. Sam's hand slipped to the back of her neck and pulled her to him. He held her like that for several seconds. Just holding her. She closed her eyes, inhaled deeply, and listened to the beating of his heart. As she slid her arms around his waist, she felt his shaft harden and press against her stomach. It sent a jolt of desire coursing through her, and from the way he started to pull away, she knew he knew what she felt.

This time things were different, and instead of pouncing on him, Malia leaned back just a little bit and reached up to caress his stubbled cheek. He didn't move away this time, but he didn't advance either. She tilted her head, offering up a small smile. "Do you want to kiss me, Sam?"

"You know I do."

That made the pressure building in her chest ease a bit. "Well?"

He leaned down and gently brushed his lips against hers. Malia rose up on her tippy toes, but Sam took a step back and shook his head. She blew out a frustrated breath. "You do know that Reagan says I'm not trying to overcompensate now. This isn't me acting recklessly."

"I don't want to hurt you, Malia."

"You won't."

Sam tugged her to him again, and this time kissed her hard. His grip on her tightened, and she met his every move with one of her own. Arms wrapping around his neck to draw him closer, running her leg up his until he gripped it with his free hand and squeezed her thigh. His scent drove her wild, and the feel of his mouth against her made her head spin.

Before she could savor the moment, his mouth had moved to her neck, leaving a cooling trail of kisses down to her shoulder. He picked her up and sat her on the counter, but his mouth never stopped its wicked decent as he tugged her tank top strap off her shoulder. Malia wrapped her legs around his waist, squeezing and pulling him closer, tangling her hands in his hair and panting.

Anticipation boiled, ramping up her arousal, at this point, she feared she'd lose her mind by the time he actually touched her. He'd moved back to her neck, but his kisses had stopped. Instead, he held her there, breathing against her neck as she kept her grip tangled in his hair. "Malia, we can't do this."

She blinked. "What? Why not?"

"Like I said—"

"No," she interrupted. "No, you don't get to use not hurting me as an excuse this time." She ran her hand down to his jeans and cupped him through the fabric. "You want me, I want you, so tell me the truth. What is really going on here?"

"Okay." He tried to take a step back, but Malia tightened her legs around him. "I just think we should take things slow."

"Slow?" She balled up her fists. "Any slower and we'd be going in reverse, Sam."

He laughed. "I just mean, the actual sleeping together. We shouldn't rush it."

"Okay," She eyed him suspiciously. There was something more, and Malia knew it. "So, this," she leaned down and kissed his neck before pulling back and meeting his gaze once more, "Is okay?" When he nodded, she slipped her hand into his jeans and ran her hand over his shaft. "But this isn't?"

His eyes squeezed shut, and his body offered up a shudder as his response. She rubbed him again and delighted in the mixed sound of pleasure and torture he made. Malia went to rub him again, but he caught her hand and pulled it away. His voice was ragged as if trying to restrain something. "Not okay, Malia," he ground out.

"Why? You liked it."

"More than you could know. You are all I think about, day in day out. While I'm out there hunting for answers, I want them so that I can come home and tell you. While I'm downstairs working in the bookshop, all I want is to run up here and taste you." She licked her lips at that, and he caught her mouth with his in a rough kiss. "But I'm trying to be noble here, to be the good guy. The white knight."

"I don't want a white knight, Sam. I just want you."

"You have me. I just need you to be patient."

"How about this," she reached down and pulled her shirt over her head causing him to groan. "You let me try my best to convince you otherwise, and we see who has better fortitude."

He'd cupped her breasts before she'd even finished, lowering his mouth to taste her. He kissed the swell and then tugged the bra down to flick his tongue over her nipple. It puckered in response, and he nipped playfully before moving to the other one. Malia leaned her head back and scooted to the edge of the counter. His shaft pressed against her entrance; fabric and jeans still separated them and yet she could still feel him. It made her core ache.

Just as she was starting to rock against him, a string of coughs echoed down the short hallway. Both of them froze and stared towards the bedrooms. There was quiet for a second and then another coughing fit. Sam leaped back, and Malia threw on her top. Both of them raced to Ellie's room to find her sitting up in bed, white as a ghost, and dripping sweat.

Malia crawled up on the bed to hold Ellie while Sam gathered up the meds Rem's doctor had given them, the bucket, and some more water. She smiled over at him as he sat on the other side of Ellie, rubbing her back and holding the bucket for the little girl as dinner revisited her. He smiled back; this was their nightly routine. Both of them sitting up with Ellie, soothing her, caring for her, and that offered some contentment. He was more than happy to be making out with her one minute and the next he was pulling dad duty to the sick child who showed no signs of getting better.

Ellie finally settled back down with Malia lying in bed next to her as Sam began reading the next chapter in a book Ellie had picked out days earlier. Sam read for hours every night, staying up with Ellie when Malia was in desperate need of sleep. She'd have to ask him one of these days when he found time to sleep. To the best of her knowledge, the only sleep he seemed to get was the few hours when he'd crash out on the couch before having to open the bookstore. She yawned and smiled over at him. He paused his reading and whispered, "Good night," to her. Ellie snuggled closer to him and laughed as he spun the tale of Alice, and Malia drifted off to sleep.

CHAPTER FIVE

Sam woke on the couch with Malia tucked in next to him. The last thing he could remember was sitting down after making a pot of coffee. They'd both been exhausted by the time Ellie's coughing had settled down, and he'd started a pot to help keep him awake long enough to go through the newest batch of emails from Rem.

Sitting up, he carefully moved Malia's head to his lap and then moved his laptop to the arm of the couch. He'd never even gotten a chance to read them before he'd passed out, and the distinct smell of scorched coffee filled the room. Rem's notes were a mess. Every source the man spoke to had contradicting stories. From a quick scan of things, Sam figured Rem would keep searching, and he would have to tell Malia that they'd hit another dead end.

An alarm on his phone dinged, and Sam slid off the couch without disturbing Malia and took another dose of meds into Ellie. "Good morning, time for some medicine."

The little girl sat up, her color had improved since last night, but Sam knew it was only a matter of time before it drained again leaving the child in pain. "I really hate that stuff."

"I know."

"It tastes terrible."

Sam poured the syrup into a measuring cup and gave it a whiff. It smelled awful; he didn't want to imagine what it tasted like. "I know, but it helps." She offered him a dull stare. It didn't work, and they both knew it was only a matter of time until the small bit of help it offered would no longer be enough. "It helps a little bit."

She nodded and took the medicine without any more hesitation. After she swallowed, she wiped her mouth with the back of her hand. "Is Malia sleeping?"

"Yeah, she fell asleep on the couch."

"With you." Ellie giggled.

He raised a brow and laughed. "Did you wake up before me?"

Ellie giggled. "She likes you." He nodded, and Ellie pressed, "You like her?"

"Very much so," he replied.

Ellie looked around. "Do I have to go live somewhere else?"

He kneeled down at the side of the bed and patted her hand. "Why would you think that?"

"I don't know."

"You're a lot like Malia, you know that?"

She smiled and looked up. "I am?"

"Yep, and I enjoy having both of you around, I don't want you to go anywhere." Tapping her under the chin, he added, "Malia is your family, this apartment is your home now. I know it's not much, but it's yours. Neither of you has to go anywhere."

"What about you?"

"You know, since you two moved in this is probably the most amount of time I've spent in my own apartment. Most of the time I'd fall asleep in the office and only run up here to grab some food. So, don't worry about me. You focus on getting better."

"I don't want to die, Sam."

His mouth went dry. Nothing he could say would make it better, and if he told her she wouldn't die that would be a lie. He opened his mouth to say something, anything that was reassuring, but instead, Malia cleared her throat from the doorway. "We are doing everything we can to make sure that doesn't happen."

"But it still might," Ellie pressed.

Malia hopped up on the bed and wrapped her arm around Ellie. Sam smiled up at both of them. These two had flipped his life completely upside down, and yet this was the most like home his apartment had ever felt, and he wouldn't want it any other way. Malia pressed her cheek against Ellie's forehead. "We'll figure something out, but for now, let's watch some cartoons."

Sam stood up and handed Ellie the remote for the TV mounted on the wall. "I'm going to go open the bookstore. If you need anything just holler."

They'd both given him a wave on his way out the door, and by the time his feet hit the landing at the bottom of the stairs his phone was ringing. Without looking at the screen, he answered it and laughed. "Need something already?"

Bast's voice greeted him instead of Malia's, "Smug this morning, aren't you?"

"Sorry, thought you were someone else. What do you need, Bast?"

"Just checking in on you. Mary's been missing for a few weeks now, you were sent out to find out what happened and I've yet to hear from you. In fact, my sources say you have barely left your shop. Is there something I should know about?"

"Do you seriously have people following me?"

"When you become unreliable to the tribe you become a liability."

"I'm not unreliable."

"Then whoever you're hiding in your apartment is the liability. Get rid of them."

"No. I'm not one of your followers. I am part of this tribe to help the others, not because I need you." Sam flipped the open sign over and made his way behind the counter. "What I do in my home is my business, so, if you want me to keep helping, then I suggest you understand that I do not work for you. I work with you and only because I choose to."

"Where's Mary?"

"The Agency has her; if she's still alive, I'll find a way to get her out." Before Bast could speak, Sam added, "They tried to get her to flip on us, but she managed to give me a heads up before they took her."

"And you just left her to die?"

"There was no way to stop it, and I can infiltrate a lot of places but the Agency's holding cells in their division building isn't one of them. I've got a contact on the inside, as of a few days ago Mary was still alive. He's working on getting her out."

"If you fail to save her, I will expel you from our family and make sure the Agency takes your head."

"Good luck with that, Bast. I have survived on my own longer than this tribe has been around. I know how to stay alive. How well will you do without me?"

A click answered Sam as the line went dead.

Rolling his eyes, he pocketed his phone and settled into his day. Bast's call shook him, and it settled in the back of his mind. The leader of their tribe spied on him and knew he had people staying with him. Sam made a mental note to call Remus and inform him that Malia and Ellie might not be safe with him anymore, but by the time he flipped the closed sign over all he really wanted to do was head upstairs and spend the rest of his night with them. As he entered his office and flipped on the light, Rem greeted him with a smile from behind Sam's desk. "Jesus, Rem. How long have you been here?"

The man's swirling eyes glanced over the piles of newspapers and maps. Two piles sat on the desk, one stack was focused on finding Mary, the other had all the information Sam had gathered on the Agency and where they might be keeping the drug making Ellie sick. "Long enough to figure out you've been very busy since last we talked. Care to explain?"

"Ellie's not getting better. I figured that I'd look around in case you came up empty-handed."

Rem laughed. "And when have you ever known me to come up empty?"

"Fair enough. So, what've you found out?"

Rem's face fell. "Actually," he scratched his head a bit, "So far, I guess you could say, I have actually come up with nothing."

Sam blew out a breath. "Well, it's a good thing I've been doing some digging. Not to mention, the Agent you put me in contact with has been able to help a little bit."

"Have you shown Malia any of this?"

"No, I don't want to get her hopes up until we have something concrete."

"Good call." Rem moved out from behind the desk and tossed a bottle at Sam. "You know that girl is going to die." Sam hung his head. He didn't want to think about it, but he knew, and he knew there was nothing he could do to stop it.

As if reading his thoughts Rem said, "You know you could fix her."

"No, there's no illness, no disease to devour. She's one of those few people who I can't help."

"Yes, you can."

Sam watched Rem's eyes swirl violently and shook his head. "I can't turn her."

"Why not?"

"Is this a life you'd wish on anyone, let alone a child?"

"Ghouls have children, and they grow up just fine."

Sam's brow drew together in a tight line. "Because they're normal until they complete puberty. Then it's survival time."

"And with a tribe helping, they thrive without ever having to fear going insane or accidentally killing a human."

"How do you think Malia would feel about it if I turned her daughter into a monster?"

"You're not a monster."

"No, vampires aren't monsters, werewolves aren't monsters. Hell, even incubi aren't seen as monsters, but humans and everyone else still tell their kids bedtimes stories of ghouls coming to eat them if they misbehave. I will never turn anyone; I will never have children. I can't put someone else in that position."

Rem stared off, just past Sam's right shoulder. For several long seconds the room was completely silent, and then Rem nodded as if answering some silent voice and focused on Sam. "And what if the time comes when you have no other choice?"

"There's always a choice, Rem."

The older man took a deep breath. "You'll have to do what you think is right. So, what is going on with Bast?"

"He's been spying on me. He knows I've got people here, and he's threatening to turn me in to the Agency if I don't deliver Mary to him. You'll need to find a new safe place for them. If Bast thinks they are a problem, he's going to try to harm them."

"And what would you do if he came after them?"

Sam narrowed his eyes. Just the thought of someone trying to hurt Ellie or Malia stirred the primal monster inside him. His vision started to cloud over with a red film, and he blinked trying to rein in his emotions. "I would kill anyone who tried."

"Hmmm." Rem smirked. "I don't know why you fight your nature, Samuel. You are their lead—"

"No, Bast is their leader. The Black King died, there isn't a successor to that throne, and even if there were, I wouldn't want it."

"Embrace who you are, before it's too late."

Some days the fortune-telling routine grated more than usual, and Sam snapped, "Too late for what?"

"Deep down you know what." Walking past Sam, Rem clasped him on the shoulder and whispered, "Take what is yours and be the leader your people need before Bast destroys everything for the ghouls."

Without any further discussion, Rem was gone, and Sam stood in the quiet office alone. Taking several long, deep breaths, he waited for the red to dissipate. The jagged points of his teeth and his claw-tipped fingertips all receded, and when he was certain his appearance was passable for human, he shut off the lights and headed upstairs.

CHAPTER SIX

"I'll clean up," Malia said with a smile as she smacked Sam's hand away from the plates on the bar. "Besides you barely touched your food."

"You sure? I do know how to wash dishes."

She shook her head and went to the sink, rinsing off the plates and stacking them in the dishwasher. "You just relax. I've got this." Shutting the dishwasher door, she turned and looked him up and down. "Are you sure you're not still hungry?"

"No, I'm good, I snack a lot during the day." Malia wrinkled her brow and pursed her lips. He came around the bar and swept her up against him. She got the distinct impression that he wanted to change the subject when he motioned toward the dishwasher and said, "I hope you're not doing this because you think you have to earn your keep around here." She didn't answer and avoided his gaze, causing him to tighten his arm around her. She felt her knees go weak, and she looked up. "Malia, you don't have to do that. This is your home. Yours and Ellie's."

"No, Sam. It's yours."

He shook his head. "I'm downstairs. So, accept it. You have a home no strings attached."

"What if one day you don't want us around?"

He smirked. "What if one day you don't want to be around?"

"I wouldn't—"

"Neither would I. For now, make this your home and stop acting like you have to tiptoe around here as a guest."

"Okay." She smiled, and as soon as his eyes zeroed in on her mouth, she found herself biting her bottom lip. His body hardened, the feel of him pressed against her made her thighs ache. Ellie's coughing echoed down the hall, and both of them took a step back. Malia ducked her head and tucked a strand of hair behind her ear as she moved past him. "Time for more medicine," she muttered.

"I'll finish cleaning up."

Without any more protest, she made her way into Ellie's room and grabbed the medicine bottle. "I know it tastes terrible, but it does help you sleep."

Ellie wrinkled her nose. "It's gross."

"Yeah." Malia sat on the bed and held out the measuring cup as Ellie reluctantly drank the contents. "How are you feeling?"

"Tired."

"Is that all?" she pressed.

Ellie yawned. "Most of the time I just feel tired. Everything hurts, everything is hard to do."

"What's hard to do?"

"Walking to the bathroom or the living room. I think one day I'll wake up and I won't be able to walk at all. Breathing is hard too. I'm always out of breath." She took a deep breath as if on cue and coughed again. "And…" The little girl pulled her lip out. Malia gasped at the sores lining Ellie's lips. "These are new," she said. "And they hurt."

"We'll figure something out, I promise."

"But you can't promise that I'll get better," Ellie stated matter-of-factly.

"No, I can't. But I will do everything possible to try."

Ellie smiled and snuggled back down in her bed. "Malia, can I ask you something?"

"Sure, anything."

"Can I call you mom?"

Malia felt the room go ice cold. Her hands shook, and she stared down at Ellie. "Are you sure you want to? I mean, your mom was—"

"My mom tried to protect me, but she's gone now. I want to die knowing that I still have a mom who is trying to keep me safe."

Malia blinked. "Ellie, we'll figure it—"

"If you can't, if I die, I don't want to die without any family."

She nodded. There was no way she could deny Ellie this, and deep down it filled her heart. It also solidified one very important thing. She would not let Ellie die. One way or another she would figure out how to save her daughter with or without help from Sam and Remus. "I'd be honored if you called me mom."

"Good." Ellie yawned and closed her eyes as Malia leaned over and kissed the top of her head.

"Good night, sleep tight."

Ellie never said a word. The child was already fast asleep thanks to the newest medicine Remus had given them. Malia slipped out of the room and came down the hallway to find Sam sitting on the couch with his laptop open scanning what looked like maps and addresses on the screen. She tried to get a better look, but Sam jumped and turned the laptop out of view when she leaned over the bar to steal a peek.

Laughing she chided him, "Nervous, are we?"

Sam set the laptop on the coffee table and rubbed his neck. "Not used to people coming up behind me."

"What were you looking at? Did you find something?"

"Nothing concrete, just a couple of building that I think might be used by the Agency. They're in close enough proximity to the areas of town where a new drug is circulating. Most people seem to have a severe reaction to it, similar to Ellie's, except they tend to die within a day or so, some even quicker. I think they might be releasing on the streets in larger doses than what they gave you and Ellie."

"Then we need to go investigate and find that drug."

He motioned for her to join him on the couch. As soon as she sat down, Sam lightly touched her knee and smiled at her. "I will investigate, but first I'm gathering some more information. I have a contact in the Agency, and he is narrowing down the locations. As soon as I have something concrete I will go in there."

"Promise?"

"Cross my heart and—"

Malia placed her hand over his mouth and shook her head. "Okay, but I can help."

Sam shook his head. "No, I can't let anything happen to you."

"Rem doesn't have to know."

Sam leaned in dangerously close, his lips a fraction from touching her and whispered, "Rem has nothing to do with it. I want to keep you safe."

She shivered and darted her tongue out to lick her lips. "But—"

He leaned in, kissing her softly at first and then sweeping his tongue over her lips, prompting her to open for him. She reveled in the kiss. In the taste and feel of him. The warmth spread over her just by being near him. Malia tangled her hands in his hair rising to move into his lap when the light of the laptop screen caught her eye. A notification flashed, and Malia saw an address pop up before the notification went away.

Sam's hands slid under her shirt and gooseflesh pricked her skin. She gave the laptop one more glance and then turned her head to kiss down his neck.

She was hungry for him, but she was also hungry for answers. Sam was already trying to pull away as she straddled him. His thick cock pressed against her, even through their clothes she could feel him. Her hips rocked, causing him to make a feral sounding growl in response. "More of that," Malia whispered.

Sam laughed. "You seem to enjoy driving me crazy."

She smiled down at him and tugged his shirt off, tossing it across the room. For once he wasn't stopping her, and she desperately needed more of him tonight. "Sam, please, touch me."

He obeyed her command, slowly unbuttoning each snap on her blouse. When it was open, he leaned back, running his hands over every inch of exposed flesh before leaning up and kissing the swell of her breasts. His hands made quick work of her bra, and before she could demand anything more, Sam laid her back on the couch, settling between her thighs. He licked his lips, and Malia's breath hitched. He ran his hands down and tugged at her jeans, hooking the elastic of her panties along with her pants and pulling them off with a bit of help from her wiggling.

As soon as she was laid bare to him, Malia smiled and pointed at his pants. "Those need to go."

He shook his head and dipped it down to kiss her stomach. Every muscle in her body tightened. His mouth traveled lower, and Malia's back arched. She ran her hands down her body until her fingers tangled in his hair. The first touch of his mouth against her folds sent electricity sizzling through her from head to toe.

Sam's tongue darted over her clit, and her eyes widened at the explosion of sensation. He teased and licked and slid his tongue through her slick folds. She could swear she saw stars. Tasting colors, her head swam as he pressed his mouth against her, his tongue thrusting in and out making the pressure inside her build to the breaking point.

She bucked her hips, gripping his hair. Grinding against his mouth until her breath caught in her throat and heat washed over her with every quiver and contraction of her muscles. Sam kept moving between her legs, his tongue furiously licking as she bit her lip, trying to keep from crying out.

Malia's legs squeezed his head, and she could swear she heard a faint chuckle. As her orgasm subsided and she relaxed, Sam came up slowly, kissing his way up her belly. He stopped at her breasts and stared up at her. "You have no idea how much I needed that."

She smiled and felt her cheeks warm. "Me too."

Scooping her up, he laid her against him and reclined back on the couch with her naked body pressed against his bare chest. He was rock hard beneath her, and it only served to send her body into a rampant need for more. Sam lightly stroked her hair, his even breathing lulled her, and her eyes started to close.

"Sam, you need..." she whispered, but he put a finger to her lips to quiet her.

If he wasn't going to listen, then she only had one course of action. Malia slid her hand down his bare side and hooked her finger in the waist of his pants. She felt him shaking his head but choose to ignore it. She quickly unbuttoned his jeans, and her breath hitched at the sight of him. No boxer or briefs, just him. Thick and long. She licked her lips and ran her fingers down the length of him. No other fabric separated them, and Malia's mouth watered. Her other hand worked to slide his jeans further down, but Sam gripped her head with both hands and shook his head. "No, Malia. No sex."

She stared at him, stunned for a few seconds. "Are you a priest or some-thing?"

"No."

There was sadness in his eyes, something he wasn't telling her, some-thing that made him afraid, and she couldn't figure it out. "Then what is going on? We just—" she blushed and couldn't say the words, but the fact that they'd just been intimate and yet he still refused any further contact with her made her head hurt. "What is going on?"

"I just think we should go slow."

Malia narrowed her eyes. "That was not going slow."

"Sorry."

She tightened her grip on his jeans and glared. "Don't you dare apologize for what we just did."

Holding up his hands he stammered. "I—I didn't mean it that way."

"I should hope not." Leaning up, Malia nuzzled his neck. "Do you want me, Sam? Yes or no."

"I—"

Moving to his ear, she growled, "Yes, or no."

"Yes."

She ran her cheek against his and whispered, "But no sex?" His only response was a quick nod. "Care to explain?"

"I don't want to hurt you, and I don't want you to regret it."

"I wouldn't—"

This time he was the one to cut her off. "You might, one day."

"I won't, but if that's your one rule, I can live with it."

"Thank you," he replied. Kissing her way down his chest, she ran her tongue over every ripple of muscle and the multitude of silvery scars. As she nipped at his exposed hip, Sam tensed. "Malia, you just said—"

"You said no sex. I'm simply reciprocating." She looked up and winked. "It's not sex, and if you can do it, then so can I."

His hands curled in her long hair, and she felt his shaft strain and throb against her. "Good god, woman. You drive me crazy."

She took that as an invitation and dipped her head down to swirl her tongue around his tip. Sam's body gave a jerk, and she caught sight of his hands gripping the couch. A light sheen of sweat already dotted his forehead, and his body shivered. Malia smiled and took him into her mouth. Working him to the back of her throat and stroking the rest of his shaft in rhythm with her sucking.

He made little satisfying noises and bucked his hips in response, and she felt her own body starting to quiver from the excitement. Every bob of her head had him thrusting further into her mouth, deeper, and even when her eyes welled up from the strain, she kept her mouth on him. Her tongue swirling and licking every time she pulled back to tease him.

The look of pure ecstasy on his face made her want to climb on top of him and ride him until neither of them could walk, but he'd made his rule. No sex. For whatever reason, it was important to him, and she would honor it. She gave the tip of his cock a soft nip with her front teeth, and his hands came up to grip her head. Malia watched him, keeping her gaze locked on his as she slowly slid her mouth down his shaft over and over. Faster, harder, deeper. He tightened his grip on her hair with every thrust, and she felt him explode the moment he squeezed his eyes shut and his body went rigid. The hot stream of liquid arousal ignited something inside her. She wanted more. It took all of her restraint not to straddle him, to take him inside her, and feel some much-needed release. Instead, she fisted her hands in his jeans and lapped and swallowed down every drop he gave her.

His hands slowly released her hair and she collapsed against his chest. The rapid rise and fall of Sam's chest panting for a breath matched her own breathlessness. Her hand splayed over his chest as he covered them with a blanket from the back of the couch and placed a kiss on the top of her head.

She didn't say a word; he didn't offer anything. No apologies this time, they simply lay there, both catching their breath. Both savoring their release. She felt her eyes growing heavy and looked up to see Sam's eyes closed. His hand worked lazy circles over her back, which told her he wasn't asleep, simply enjoying himself.

Several minutes ticked by, and she swore she could stay like that forever. With him. Laying naked against him. Safe and sound. His hand had stopped its movement, and his breathing leveled out. Malia smiled to herself. She'd sated him. Stifling a yawn, she grinned again. He'd sated her.

Just as she closed her tired eyes, a flash lit up Sam's computer screen. Malia opened her eyes to see the notification on the right-hand side of the screen. "Address confirmed. Agency manufacturing plant. -Peterson," she read to herself.

Glancing back up, she felt a twinge of guilt seeing Sam's trusting face fast asleep. "I'm sorry," she whispered.

CHAPTER SEVEN

The guilt of leaving Sam asleep on the couch and Ellie sleeping down the hall settled as well as a lead ball in the pit of her stomach. Malia had managed to get dressed, grab a gun out of the locked gun safe Sam kept in the master bedroom, and sneak out of the house without disturbing either Sam or Ellie. She'd been certain that he'd have woken up when she fumbled his keys trying to find the one for the gun safe, but Sam had rolled over and never opened his eyes.

"Way to go, Malia," she chided herself. "I'm sure he'll really appreciate you knocking him out with a blowjob, stealing his stuff, and going out alone at night." She rolled her eyes at herself. Sam was going to protect her no matter what, which meant he wasn't going to let her look for a cure for Ellie. Regardless of his good intentions, she wasn't a damsel in distress in need of rescuing.

She almost laughed at the thought; that was exactly what she had been when they met. A damsel in distress and he was her knight, rescuing her and Ellie from that cargo container. Saving them from god-knows-what sort of terrible fate. Shaking her head, she pushed away the guilt. He didn't have to protect them anymore. As much as the guilt for leaving him tonight was eating her alive, it'd be a million times worse if Sam got hurt because of her.

As she scaled the chain-link fence around the old warehouse, a sharp edge of fencing snagged her pants. She struggled to free herself and cursed as she hit the ground. The fence tore through her pants and gouged a deep cut into her inner thigh. After a few minutes of brushing herself off and trying to stop the bleeding, Malia gave up. "It's a scratch. It'll be fine."

Prowling her way to a side window of the building, she peeked inside. Even in the darkness, she could make out rows of empty tables and stools by the faint glow emanating from a hallway on the other side of the room. Pushing the window open, she slipped inside. It hadn't escaped her that if the Agency wanted to keep people out of the building, then they would have locked the place up better, but curiosity kept her moving forward regardless of the growing tension in her gut.

Yellow lighting bathed the hallway, making her feel slightly nauseous, but she pressed forward. Every room turned out to be empty. Some had the same putrid yellow lighting; others were pitch black. Those were the rooms that made the hair on the back of her neck stand on end when she entered them, but as far as she could tell the building was a complete waste of time.

Malia found herself at a door marked Roof Access and let out a sigh. "Great." The rusty door creaked as she pushed it open. Malia took several steps forward and placed her hands on her hips, kicking at the loose gravel covering the roof. "Another dead end."

"For you? Yes," a deep voice answered from behind her. Turning slowly, Malia swallowed the lump of fear threatening to close off her throat. Red eyes beaded the darkness, and one by one, vampires dressed in Agency suits with badges stepped into the moonlight. Their pale skin, handsome, chiseled features, red eyes, and the sudden cold in the air instilled fear deep in her soul. A tall vampire with short blond hair seemed to take the lead. Unlike the other others, he didn't wear a suit jacket, simply slacks, white button shirt, tie, and a shoulder holster. Malia took another step back hoping for more distance between them so she could try to figure out what to do. His voice was lethal like a cold blade sliding over her body. "This is a dead end, my dear."

Sam awoke to the buzzing of his phone. He rubbed his eyes, taking notice that he was all alone and knowing full well when he'd fallen asleep Malia had been naked sleeping on top of him. Looking at the number, he answered, "Peterson, what's up? Why are you calling at this time of night?"

"I'm calling because you are in deep shit."

"What? Why?"

"You know, when I sent you that address tonight, I didn't expect you to go breaking into the place. We had an agreement, remember?"

Sam shook his head trying to shake the fog from his brain. "What are you talking about? Our agreement still stands, you find the addresses, confirm they are Agency, follow-up and make sure the coast is clear, and then I go in and see what I can find. But you didn't send me anything tonight."

"Yeah, I did, and I assumed the alarm someone tripped in the building I sent to you meant that you'd taken things into your own hands."

"Wait." Sam pinched the bridge of his nose. "When did you send the message? I didn't see one, and I've been asleep for," glancing at his phone he groaned, "I've been asleep for at least an hour."

He was already checking his computer when Peterson answered, "About an hour ago." Sam brought up the email and cursed. His Agency contact groaned, "What's wrong?"

"Malia." Sam cursed again and glanced around the living room. Her shoes were missing from the front door where she kept them. He stood up, buttoning his jeans and slipping on his boots as he made his way down the hallway. Ellie was still tucked into bed sleeping peacefully, but the master bedroom where he'd hoped to find Malia was empty. "Shit. She's gone out on her own."

"This is a fucking problem, man," Peterson responded.

Sam couldn't agree more. "I've got a kid here; I can't leave her alone. She's the one who's sick, but I've got to find Malia. If she's triggered the alarm she's in trouble."

"Give me your address." Sam rattled it off, and Peterson muttered something to someone else then said. "Meet us at the front door of your shop."

Without another word, Sam bolted for the door and leaped down the stairs, taking them in one jump. He landed in a crouch and sprinted to the door. As he threw it open, the werewolf he knew only as Peterson stood before him with a petite blonde woman at his side and a dark-haired vampire behind the both of them. "That was quick," Sam snorted.

"Uber's got nothing on vampires," the vamp said.

Shaking his head, Sam motioned to the store. "Stairs are at the back, thanks for this. Her name is Ellie, and if she wakes up, there is some medicine in the fridge that she can take to keep down the fever and coughing."

Before any of the newcomers could say a word, Sam was gone. He had to get to Malia before he lost everything. He'd lost it all once before; he wasn't going to lose anyone else. Not Malia. Not Ellie. The thought stunned him, and Rem's words came back to haunt him. He could save Ellie, but Malia would hate him for it. He pushed the thoughts to the back of his head. He needed a clear mind to track Malia. Luckily, he had her scent committed to memory, which led him straight to the address Peterson had sent him.

The scent of her blood rose up, and Sam's teeth sharpened. She was hurt. Or worse. Red clouded his vision as he leaped he six-foot fence in one bound and landed kneeling, hands splayed on the ground as he whipped his head from side to side to find her trail. A breeze drifted by carrying the smell of lavender and blood with it, and Sam shot a glance towards the roof.

He ran to the side of the building and jumped, catching the end of a broken fire escape with one hand and pulling himself up. The old warehouse only stood four stories tall, but every moment he was away from Malia felt like forever. His fingernails lengthened into sharp claws, and he used them to climb up the ramshackle wall when the fire escape stairs ended twenty feet from the roof. With one fluid movement, he lifted himself over the edge as soon as both hands firmly gripped the ledge.

The scene before him made his chest contract. Malia faced off a horde of vampires. Sam took note that every single one of them was an Agent, and from their blood-red eyes, he could tell they were hungry for a taste of her. Neither Malia or the group of vampires noticed him. He'd never considered the fact that Malia knew how to fight; part of him just assumed she'd need his help, but judging by the injuries on a couple of the vampires and her current warrior stance, his mate wasn't helpless.

Sam blinked at the thought. Malia wasn't his mate. She wasn't. But she was, and his gut knew it, and even more, the monster inside of him knew it and wanted to protect her. He was about to call out to her, to tell her to stop, when she charged at a blond vampire at the front of the group. Her battle cry was fierce, but Sam could see the entire event playing out in slow motion, and no amount of battle bravado could stop what was happening.

A flash of silver glinted in the moonlight, and Malia came to a stop too late. She stumbled backward, gripping the large knife buried in her side. The vampire grinned and yanked the metal out taking pieces of flesh with it. Sam's rage exploded. Everything turned red. The vampires in his vision were black silhouettes, targets to tear apart, and he tore through them before Malia had even hit the floor.

He twisted a head from one of the vampire's shoulders. Slashed the throat out of another and then leaped to catch the blond one who'd stabbed Malia. They crashed to the ground. Gravel from the rooftop bit into Sam's hands and knees, but he shrugged it off. The vampire's image started to flicker. He was getting ready to flee, and Sam couldn't allow it. With one quick scramble, Sam lunged for the vamp, catching its throat in his clawed hand. Sam tightened and ripped a chunk of flesh from the vampire who wailed in pain for a second before he teleported from the roof.

The remaining vampires fled in the same manner as their leader, and Sam whipped his head around assessing any more threats before he heard a soft gurgle coming from Malia.

"Malia!" Sam slid across the gravel lot to embrace Malia. His eyes changed back to blue, and he could see her in full color once again. His hand slid to her side, and to his horror, his hand came away coated in more than just blood. "No, no!" He sniffed his hand and yelled, "No!"

"Sam—" Her voice broke off in a string of coughs.

"Stay with me. Listen to me, please. You've been poisoned." The next words came rushing out before he could even stop to think, "I can save you, I can, but I won't do it without permission."

She focused on his face and shook her head. "What?"

"I can save you, but you'll change."

"I don't understand."

"Malia, I'm not human."

Another round of coughing made the blood spurt from the wound. "You are human. You're like me. Just human."

"No, I'm not."

"How? You're not a vamp; you're not a wolf. You can't be an incubus since you keep refusing sex." She coughed and turned her head to the side to spit out a mouthful of blood.

"I'm a monster, Malia."

"We're all some sort of monster, but you are the kindest man I know. You aren't one of them."

"Malia." He licked his lips, finding them suddenly dry and his throat closing up. "You are dying; I can smell it; I can taste it in the air. You're going to go soon."

Her eyes were wild. "Then do it, do whatever you have to." She winced again, "It hurts, Sam, I don't want to die."

Without a thought, he rolled up his sleeve and took out a knife. Her eyes pleaded without words. He made a slice across his wrist, opening it up as blood dripped into her wound. He hesitated for a moment, then used the knife to cut a strip of flesh from the same wrist. Holding it up, he swallowed hard and then moved it closer to her mouth. "Malia, I'm a ghoul."

He saw it then. The shock, the fear, the revulsion in her eyes. She tried to move back, but the wall gave her nowhere to go. "A ghoul. Oh god, no. No!"

"I won't hurt you. I swear it."

"You eat dead people. You're sick."

"No. We don't do that." He stopped, that was a lie. "I don't do that. Some ghouls do, but it's because they don't know any better. Look at me, Malia." She shuttered and turned away. The stench of death was growing stronger, every moment they wasted was one minute closer to losing her forever. He dropped the knife and gripped her chin, turning her gaze to meet him. "Malia, ghouls have evolved; we don't have to eat a whole human." He shook his head; everything was coming out wrong. "We only need to consume a small amount of living flesh, we've adapted over the centuries, we can mostly feed off of human emotions, from their essence. I don't hurt people."

"But you still have to eat them." She whimpered, "I can't—"

"We only eat from donors; they give their consent. We honor their wishes." He moved the flesh closer to her mouth, and she shook her head. "You're dying. There's no time to go over everything. Please, trust me." Tears stung his eyes. "Hate me later, just live. Take it, please. Think of Ellie; don't leave her without a mother."

Her eyes widened at his words, but she whispered, "I'll be a monster."

He winced. That stung more than he'd imagined, but it didn't matter. Her survival mattered, and his composure was slipping. Sam's vision blurred red; he didn't need a mirror to know that his eyes had changed. The whites of his eyes would be black, that black would bleed outward following the veins around his eyes, giving the illusion of a black mask, and the irises would be red. His teeth sharpened into razor sharp weapons. "Live, Malia," he demanded.

"Wha—What is happening to you?"

"I'm getting ready to hunt."

"I thought you said you don't hurt people?"

He moved the flesh against her lips. "You said you didn't want to die. You told me to do it, to save you."

"Are you going to hurt me?"

The fear in her eyes broke him to the center of his soul. "Never in a million years. You will live. Someone will teach you how to hide from the world as I did. And I swear you will have as normal a life as possible."

As she started to open her mouth, she looked down at her wound. Her eyes widened as she saw the wound starting to knit back together. "You've been turning me this whole time, haven't you?"

Sam slowly closed his eyes. The blood dripping from his wrist into her open wound would be enough to trigger the change, but consuming his flesh would seal her transition. Without it she would slowly die, her body starving for the sustenance only a creator can offer. "Like I said. Hate me later, just live." Without another word, he pressed the flesh past her lips and held her mouth closed. "Swallow it." Even to his own ears, his voice sounded cold, but she would live. He could live with her hating him, but there was no way he was letting her die.

Malia visibly worked her throat to swallow his flesh. He removed his hand, and she pushed him further away. Beautifully defiant. He couldn't help but grin. "I do hate you, Samuel, make no mistake about it."

"I'm okay with that." He stood up. "Your wound is healing already. In twenty-four hours, your transformation will be complete. I care about your survival; that's been my only concern since I found you."

"And now you're going hunting?"

"Yes."

"Who are you hunting?"

"The people responsible for harming you."

"You hurt me." She glared up at him.

He blew out a heavy breath. "Keep that anger, Malia, use it. You can hate me for a thousand years, but I will do whatever is necessary to protect you. Always."

CHAPTER EIGHT

"Three weeks, Sam," Rem's voice echoed all around the empty room.

"And she's adapting."

"And Ellie can't walk now."

Sam stilled at the news. "Last time we spoke you said she was getting better."

"I was wrong. The doctor says she has some sort of secondary infection from the drug. Whatever toxin they used in its production has even more long-lasting effects than we realized."

"How did all of this get past you? I know you have a hand in all of that Syndicate business." Rem arched a brow at Sam's declaration. "In fact, I'm pretty damn sure you run the thing. So how are you not able to heal her?"

Rem pinched the bridge of his nose. "Son, there are some things that even a demigod can't fix."

Sam's mouth fell open. "Demigod? That's what you are?" Rem nodded, and Sam's vision went red. "All these years and you never told me? What the fuck, Rem? We were—" he stopped mid-sentence and glared. "Why? Why did you save me when I was a kid, why ask me to help your granddaughter? And why in the hell didn't you tell me who the hell you were?"

"Listen, son."

Sam bristled at the word and snarled, "Call me son one more time!"

Rem held up his hand. "I saw greatness in you. The potential to lead your people."

"They aren't my people. I am not their leader."

"You are, and in the legend, the Black King has his queen by his side."

Sam shrugged. "Malia isn't the Black Queen."

"Oh?" Rem arched a brow and pulled out his cell phone. After punching in something, he turned the phone around for Sam to see a local newscast.

The reporter stood outside a crime scene holding her microphone in a trembling hand. "We don't know who or what is responsible for the four dead vampires found inside, but some bystanders happened to record footage of the attack. Authorities are asking anyone who might know the assailant to please contact them immediately." The feed cut to a grainy video of a woman with long brown hair and red eyes attacking the vampires in a fluid acrobatic attack that left them all headless in the short span of forty-five seconds. The red eyes weren't the glowing ones of a vampire. The whites were black, the skin around her eyes looked like a black mask, but it wasn't a mask, it was the change in skin pigmentation that only showed up in one specific bloodline of ghoul, and her irises were red. Just like his. And it was a red he was all too familiar with. The red that meant someone, or in this case, multiple someones, were going to die.

His eyes turned and his teeth sharpened in response to her wildness. He wanted her. He wanted to taste her, touch her, fuck her, hunt with her, and roll around in a pool of blood with her just to do it all over again. Sam shook his head. "Who's seen this?"

"The entire city by now. Your tribe, for sure. Probably half the world at the rate that humans share shit on the internet."

"What am I supposed to do? She hates me, Rem."

"Make her face you. Don't give her the option to push you away. Ellie needs you. She asks for you constantly. They both need you."

He shook his head. "I did what she wanted; I walked away after that night."

"You left her everything, your store, your apartment. Now you are over here in the vampire district living like a vagrant in an apartment that's barely up to code. Why did you give her everything?"

"Because I took everything from her when I changed her."

"And now she's alive," Rem countered. "She is here, so stop being a fucking pussy and go get her. Help her; she is spiraling out of control. She's rebellious. Refuses to listen. Sound familiar?"

It did. Sam was the same way after Rem had cured the insanity of his mind. It was only with the help of the siren he'd employed that Sam began to come around, and that was mostly due to the influence of the siren's song that kept him in a less agitated state until Rem could impress upon him how to be civilized. "You helped me, why not help her?"

"You know why, son." Sam shook his head, and Rem said, "I may be her family, but you are her mate. She is forever bound to you and you to her. So, fix this."

The bell dinged as Sam pushed open the front door of the bookstore. Everything seemed brighter in the shop. More light poured in from the windows; a few people looked up from their reading to see who had entered the store. They seemed uninterested in him and returned to their books. Malia was nearby. He could smell her, which meant she'd probably picked up his scent too. He flexed his hands, preparing for a battle with his wild mate.

"Come to pick up something to read?" she asked from the darkness of one of the aisles.

Sam cautiously stepped around the corner and advanced to where she stood at the back of the shop. "I came to see you."

"Why?" Even in the low light, he could see her glance awkwardly at her feet to avoid his gaze. "You left."

"You didn't want me around."

"I was scared," she countered.

He rubbed the back of his neck. "I'm sorry."

"You changed me before you'd explained what you were."

"The blood was only a temporary fix. You wouldn't have transformed until you consumed your maker's flesh." He narrowed his gaze. "And to be honest, I'd do it all again if given the chance so that Ellie didn't lose you. Your daughter needs you."

"And now she's even worse. So, what are we going to do?"

"We aren't doing shit, Malia. Look at what happened last time you tried to do something. You got yourself killed."

"I didn't die." She defiantly thrust her chin in the air. "Remember?"

"Yeah, I remember," his voice rose, and he could hear the sound of shuffling in the front of the shop.

Malia stomped her foot and turned down the aisle. "Sorry," she called out to the shoppers. "The shop is closing early. Feel free to come back tomorrow." He'd made his way out of the bookshelves and leaned against the counter as she finished ushering customers out. When the lock clicked into place, Malia closed the blinds over the window and proceeded to pull the curtains to cover the large display window in the store, then she whirled around and pinned him with a glare. "Unlike last time I can hold my own."

"Let's talk about last time, shall we?" He pointed at her. Malia crossed her arms over her chest and shrugged, sending Sam into a near rage. "You gave me a blowjob, waited for me to fall asleep, got into my laptop, read my email, and took off on your own to face the Agency. Then when I finally get there, I find you dying. I'm not about to watch something else happen to you."

"First off, I didn't plan for any of that to happen and I didn't get into your laptop. A notification popped up, and I read it. It said that the building was confirmed as an Agency building. I acted on instinct."

"Your instinct got you killed!" he blurted out.

"Almost killed. I survived. Which is something you seem to keep over-looking."

"You know what I mean, Malia."

"I'm stronger and faster now. I can hold my own."

"Except for the fact that you got caught, and rule number one about being a ghoul is never, ever get caught."

Her face paled, and eyes widened. "Caught?"

"You don't know?" He stepped closer, took out his phone, and cued up the news report. "The humans have seen you. They don't know what you are because we've kept ourselves hidden for all these years. Now they are hunting for some new threat that might eventually lead them right to our tribe."

"What's a tribe?" she asked.

Sam pinched the bridge of his nose and counted to ten. The frustration was building to a head, and he had no one to blame but himself. Just as he was about to open his mouth, the familiar voice of Bast came from behind him. "The tribe is your home, my Queen."

Sam turned slowly and stared at Bast fully bowing before Malia and shook his head. "She isn't your queen, you idiot."

"We've seen the video, Samuel. All this time we'd been keeping an eye out for the Black King, some of us actually thought it might be you, but I suppose the legend had it all wrong. It wasn't a king who was the next in line; it was a queen." Bast paused and pointed a finger at Sam, "You hid her from us; you tried to keep her from her people, from her tribe."

Sam looked at the ceiling and gritted his teeth. "She isn't the descendant of Al-Malik al-Aswad."

"You continue to insult our culture, Samuel. We do not refer to the Black King by his name. At every turn, you show disrespect." Turing to Malia he bowed again. "It is my humble honor to welcome you home, my queen. I am the leader of our tribe. You may call on me in any capacity, and since you are new to our colony, I would offer my services to continue as leader of our people and sit at your right hand. I can't imagine how you've survived so long on your own."

Sam growled. There was no way in this life or another that he would allow Bast to sit at Malia's side. Malia looked at Sam and back to Bast, eyes still wide and innocent. Sam cursed himself for putting her in this situation and stepped between them, "She doesn't need your help—"

Bast cut him off, "I also ask that you banish this traitor. Samuel offers nothing to our society; he is a relic from the past, a child pretending to be a man, who tried to hide you from us. Death would be a suitable punishment for such treason, but I can see you have a kind heart. Banish him to show your power to the tribe."

Malia placed a hand on Sam's shoulder and moved past him. She held her head high, and Sam couldn't help but smile at just how damn regal she looked playing the part. "Thank you for your offer and your suggestion." She looked back at Sam, giving him a small smile and then turned to Bast. "If I am your queen then it wouldn't be right to rush to judgment at this moment. I will need some time to contemplate what I should do with traitors and whom I might take as my councel, but," she held up her hand, "I will need to confer with Samuel. He seems very adamant that you are mistaken in my identity."

"He cannot be trusted. He will lie to you."

Malia glared. "If I am this Black Queen you say I am, then isn't it an insult to imply that someone lesser than I could so easily manipulate me?"

Sam grinned. She could play this role very well if given the chance. Her command of Bast was proof that even when thrown into the deep end, Malia would swim rather than sink and maybe, just maybe, he hadn't given her enough credit. After a few more complaints, Bast tucked tail and left through the back entrance leaving Sam alone with his mate.

This time he did not say a word. Before she'd fully turned around, he rushed her, slamming them both against the solid end of the nearest bookshelf. He pinned her arms above her head, and his mouth claimed her just as she whispered his name. Her tongue met his with fury. Passion exploded between them. No more tender touches and sweet words. She could take his strength, match it, and dole out her own punishments. And he welcomed them.

When he released her hands, Malia tore at his shirt, ripping it to shreds with her claws, and her sharp teeth nipped at his shoulder. He had her naked within seconds of breaking the kiss. She panted and tangled her hands in his hair. Every inch of him responded to her need. Her skin against his lips made him burn; her scent drove him crazy. Sam ran one hand down her stomach. Cupping her sex, he ground his palm against her bundle of nerves and delighted in the sounds she made. His mouth found the hollow of her neck, and he scraped his sharp teeth over her flesh.

She instantly wrapped one leg around his hip, and Sam took pleasure in sinking his fingers deep inside her. Malia struggled to yank his pants off as she rode his hand, but as soon as his cock was free, he felt her muscles tighten. The tip throbbed and rested against her folds while he kept working his fingers, making her quiver. The look of pure pleasure on her face filled him with pride. She was his queen, no one else's, and he'd spend eternity like this with her if she'd let him.

"More," she whispered.

It was a command he intended to obey. Sliding his fingers out he stroked himself with her slick arousal and lifted her slightly to bury himself inside her tight core. Every thrust sent books crashing to the ground, the wood of the bookcase groaned in protest. He watched her as she reached back to grip the shelf for support. Her heaving breasts bounced every time he pistoned his hips. The sheen of sweat covering her naked body and the way her petite claws clamped and sunk into the antique wood of the bookshelf only encouraged him to drive himself deeper.

Those marks on the shelf would stay. They'd be a reminder of how he claimed his mate. His mouth crashed into her to silence her moans. Sam's hands traveled up her sides, up her arms, and encircled her wrists once more to hold her right where he wanted her. Malia's legs wrapped tightly around his waist, and he felt the tightness start. Her walls clenched his cock. The rhythmic quivers matched his throbbing need for release. He was so close. As she snagged his lower lip with sharpened teeth and bit, blood rushed from his lip, and Malia's body turned feverish.

She bucked wildly, and his cock swelled. Nothing had felt so blindingly hot before. Her ferocious sucking of his lip sent ripples of tension colliding with building pressure. Her core squeezed around his shaft, and Sam came undone. He pumped harder, faster, burying himself to the hilt as she finally released his lip. Blood scented the room, it dripped from her chin, and her eyes had turned red. To his astonishment, he hadn't noticed that his vision was clouded with crimson as well. It was different this time. He hadn't noticed because he could see her in color. Everything else was red, but Malia was vibrant and beautifully untamed. His release filled her, and her body answered with screams that broke from her lips as her tight walls quivered and milked every last drop from him.

When he could finally catch his breath, Sam inhaled sharply and rested his forehead against her chest. He was still holding her up, bracing most of their weight against the bookshelf for leverage, but even then, he could feel the strain on his muscles as they burned. She wrapped her arms around his neck and rested her cheek against the top of his head. "Sam... Don't ever leave me alone again."

"I won't. I promise." Slowly he lowered her to the ground and steadied her on her feet. Pulling his jeans on and fastening them, Sam quickly dismissed the torn shirt. "Stay here," he insisted as he excused himself and headed to his office. When he came back into the room, he handed her a fresh shirt and let his eyes drink in the sight of her as she got dressed. She seemed to be sizing him up as well. He noted how her eyes traveled up and down his chest, settling on the waist of his low-slung jeans. A smile played on his lips as he relaxed in one of the many chairs scattered around the store. Nervous energy emanated from her, and as soon as she started twisting her hands in the hem of the shirt, Sam leaned forward. "What is it?"

She shrugged. "Why haven't you told them yet?"

"Told who, what?"

Malia's hips swayed as she made her way over to the chair and straddled him. "That you are their king."

"I'm not," he answered flatly.

"You are. You told that man that I was not a descendant of whoever this Black King is, but he seems to think I am because of my eyes."

"And?" He gripped her hips and tugged her closer in his lap.

She blushed. "I saw your eyes just now. They are like mine. There's only one reason I'd have eyes like that."

A tick worked in his jaw. "I'm not their king."

"You are." Her voice rose up, "I got my eyes from my maker, didn't I? And you are my maker. You are a leader. Take your place and lead them."

"You don't know what you are asking."

"I'm not asking anything, Samuel. I'm demanding my king take his place and lead our people."

His eyes changed, and he shivered when hers changed in response. Blowing out a heavy sigh, he held his head in his hands. "Being king and queen got my parents killed. Ghouls like Bast, who think we should stay isolated, separate from the world, who don't condone our current feeding habits, ghouls who want to take what we need without permission. Ghouls who want to kill. They killed my parents because my parents preached this new lifestyle of interaction, peace, and sustaining ourselves through emotions rather than flesh. It took me a long time to figure out what had happened to my parents, even longer for me to come to terms with the fact that I am the last descendant of Al-Malik al-Aswad. I never wanted to pass this legacy to another generation."

He looked up to see tears shimmering in her eyes. Malia's voice cracked, "And now?"

"I'll do anything in my power to keep you safe."

"What about passing on your legacy?"

He stared at her for several seconds but couldn't form the words. Yes. He wanted children. He wanted a family. But the price was too high. Bast was ruthless and would do anything to keep his power. "We need to check on Ellie," he finally said to change the subject.

Malia hopped off his lap. "Reagan has been staying with her during the day while I run the store. I'm sure she's keeping Ellie entertained."

"I've missed you both."

She looked up at him through thick lashes and whispered, "We've missed you too."

Malia sat at the table with Reagan waiting for Sam. They'd spent all evening in Ellie's room. Malia's heart had broken into a million pieces seeing how happy Ellie was to see him. She'd been a fool to lash out at him the night he'd saved her. He'd even told her she'd hate him for it and yet she'd still told him to do it. Then like an even bigger fool, she'd taken out all of her fear and anger on him and sent him away.

Reagan cleared her throat and said, "Malia, don't dwell on the past."

"Easy for you to say, I pushed him away."

"You were scared. It's understandable. Have you worked on your hunger issues?" Reagan jerked her head towards the hallway and added, "Or told him about it?"

She shook her head. "How can I tell him I'm an unstoppable eating machine?"

"You simply be honest and tell him, you don't know how to feed on emotions, and you can't control your hunger. He will understand."

"Will he? Sam's already concerned about my safety. He's pissed that I exposed his people by being caught on video. How's he going to react knowing that I killed those vampires to feed on them because I'm constantly hungry."

"You're hungry because you're feeding on the undead and it's going to turn you insane if you don't stop," Sam's voice sent a chill down her spine.

Reagan coughed and slid her chair back. "I think that's my cue to go. How's Ellie?"

"Burning up again," Sam answered.

Something dark crossed over his face, and Malia sniffed the air recoiling at the stench. "Oh god, what is that smell?"

"Death," Sam whispered. "She's dying, Malia."

Reagan paused and looked at Malia. "You two need to do something. Find something to use as an antidote."

Malia looked at Sam as tears stung her eyes. "What can we do?"

"We have to go out. We have to hunt the Agency down and get a sample of that drug. Rem," he paused and corrected himself with a touch of disdain in his voice, "Remus should be able to figure out something if we can get a pure sample."

She blinked. "You know about Rem's true identity?"

Sam silently waited as Reagan proceeded to pull out her phone and excuse herself while she probed whoever was on the other line for answers. When she was gone, he finally spoke, "It took a bit of digging but yeah," he said coolly, "I know all about how my friend and mentor Rem is actually the demigod Remus who leads the Syndicate."

"You're hurt?" She advanced and wrapped her arms around him.

He didn't say a word; he didn't have to. She could feel the pain emanating from of him. Malia stood up and wrung her hands nervously. "I'm helping with this; don't tell me I have to stay."

"I won't. I'll need you. Your speed almost matches mine; we're faster than most of our kind, which is saying something because true ghouls can give a werewolf a run for their money. But," he held up his hand, "You stay by my side, we fight as a team, and we are in and out as quick as possible. Ellie's breathing is growing shallow, I can feel the necrosis of death creeping in, and I won't lose either of you."

"Will an antidote work?"

"I hope so."

She licked her lips. "And if it doesn't?"

He shook his head. "It will have to."

"Remus said that ghouls eat the sickness out of people, that you ask permission of the dying to help by curing them. Why can't you do that for her?"

"Because she doesn't have a disease or a curable illness. There's something killing her that I can't remove. I can taste it; it's everywhere, and yet when I try to locate it, it's nowhere. This thing that is taking her away from us isn't a normal illness; it's supernatural, and the only hope we have is for Remus and his Syndicate people to find a cure."

Sam took a step toward the door, but Malia touched his bicep, and he stilled. "Sam, I wish I could have told you about Remus."

"I understand your loyalties to him. You are his granddaughter after all."

"Great, great, great, etcetera," she added.

"Blood is blood, Malia."

She cupped his chin, staring into his eyes. "It's not thicker than us. You, me, and Ellie. We are a family, and nothing and no one is coming between us. Not even blood."

CHAPTER NINE

Reagan's contacts within the Agency had finally pointed them to their freshest lead all night. After three abandoned sites, the fourth one was a win. Malia took the instructions on combat and hunting Sam had given her over the course of hours they'd been out looking for answers and applied them with an aptitude that astonished her. She'd always been a fast learner and a decent fighter from growing up alone, but her new skills and the ability to execute them left her feeling like she was unstoppable.

Something slammed into her from the shadows, and the glow of red vampire eyes quickly let her know that she was, in fact, not unstoppable. It was a mistake she wouldn't make again. The vampire's attack was sloppy; his first swing sent him off balance, and Malia jumped on his back, sunk her teeth into his neck and shoulder, and tore out a chunk.

"Don't swallow it," Sam warned.

She spat out the chunk and let the body drop to the ground. Dead vampires littered their path by the time they made their way into a makeshift laboratory. Malia's eyes burned from the vapors and chemicals in the room. "What do we look for?"

The red killing haze had left her eyes, and the world around them came rushing back in full color. Sam shook his head. "Grab samples of anything that looks important. We won't know what to look for; might as well be safe and take everything we can find."

Opening the backpack she'd kept strapped to her back, Malia filled it will any sealed vials she could find. When there were no more samples, she took to shoving papers filled with calculations and formulas into the pack. Sam was busy on the other side of the room doing the same, and five minutes later they stood at the door, backpacks full, and a hum of energy in the air.

Sam narrowed his eyes as they stepped out of the room and into the hallway now teeming with vampires. Malia caught a glance at his menacing look before he slipped past her. She came up behind him and stilled. The blond vampire who'd stabbed her stood at the head of the pack. She tugged on Sam's arm, but he didn't give her a second look. His gaze was locked on the blond vampire. Malia's gut twisted. He was going for revenge.

Movements in all directions blurred her vision. Panic swelled up in her chest. Sam was going straight for the vampire who'd hurt her. All the others were trying to swarm him before he could reach their leader, and Malia found herself frozen with fear. What was different about facing these vampires as opposed to the ones they'd already taken out?

"Sam," she whispered.

He would be willing to die to avenge her, and the smug smile on the vamp's face said he was ready for anything Sam could dole out. Something clicked just then in her brain, and her body moved on autopilot as she leaped from one vampire to another, breaking necks, ripping out throats, and rushing to another target as soon as one would fall. She couldn't focus on Sam and the blond vampire. She had to protect her mate from the others coming for his back.

When the vamps behind Sam were nothing but a pile, she whipped her head around to see how her mate was doing. He was slashing and gnashing his teeth at the vampire who was more on the retreat than trying to defend himself. She chalked it up to the fact that more than likely they'd never faced off with cognizant ghouls before. The Black King was far from a mindless monster. He was speed and grace and death all wrapped into one. As the vampire stumbled into the roof access door, he called out, "Secure the sample! Don't let them leave with it."

A group of vampires materialized down the corridor and bolted straight toward Malia. She braced herself for a fight, but the six vampires rushed past her and headed for the lab. Sam yelled, "Malia, get to it first. Kill them all!"

She sprinted after them. They were going berserk in the lab, tearing it apart. She hadn't seen anything other than what they'd already taken, but the vampires were opening hidden storage she hadn't found when they searched. Grabbing one vampire by the shoulder as he tried to rush past her, Malia growled in his ear, "Where's the sample?"

"You'll never find it, freak."

She bared her sharp teeth and snapped them near his neck. "Do you want to die?"

"Kill me," he hissed.

Malia popped her jaw and widened her mouth, and the vampire's eyes widened. His pleas died on his lips before he could summon the words. She'd bitten clean through his neck, severed the spinal cord, and took satisfaction in the sound of silence that met her ears. Wiping her mouth on the back of her hand, she turned to find the five remaining vampires coming at her.

Their attacks were swifter than she expected. Fists pummeled her face and body. Claws cut her open to the bone, and their fangs sank deep into every inch of skin they could latch onto. Her world went dark, and the cold chill of the linoleum floor was the last sensation she felt.

"Malia, wake up."

Sam's voice rattled in her head as she opened her eyes. The stinging smell of the lab greeted her, and she found herself lying in Sam's bloody lap. "What happened?"

"They're gone."

She sat up and saw four extra bodies on the ground and a detached arm and leg. "Where'd the rest of them go?"

"The last two fled with their commander."

She swallowed. "The blond vampire? He got away?"

Sam looked away but nodded.

Malia cupped his cheek and leaned up to kiss him deeply. He returned the kiss, but his body was still stiff. "Don't be angry; he'll get what's coming to him," Malia promised.

Sam pointed to the arm and leg. "He'll be missing these, and as far as I know, vampires can't regenerate whole limbs, at least not without decades of healing, so regardless, he'll remember this fight."

She smiled. "What about this sample he wanted?"

Sam held up a vile labeled "Specimen 21" and pointed to a hidden safe in the wall that now stood open. "The vampires had already opened it up by the time I'd gotten in here."

"We have the cure?" she asked excitedly.

Sam smiled. "I hope so. Let's go; your wounds are almost completely healed now. Ellie and Reagan are waiting for us."

When they exited the building, Sam helped her to the car they'd been scouting sites in and drove back to the bookstore to find all the lights in the building blazing. Malia wrinkled her brow. "Did we leave the lights on?"

Sam shook his. "This can't be good."

After parking and gathering up their packs, both of them charged up the stairs and swung open the apartment door to find Reagan and Remus standing in the kitchen with a half dozen other people. One woman stood out, her golden hair flowed over her shoulders, and piercing green eyes stayed locked on Sam. Her angular features were drawn tight. Malia leaned over and whispered, "Do you know her?"

"Yes," he answered and stepped forward. "You're the siren, right?"

The woman bowed her head, and her sing-song voice made Malia's arms break out in gooseflesh. "I am. I didn't think you'd remember me, Samuel." She bowed to Malia. "I'm pleased to see you found your queen."

"I did." He didn't protest this time, and Malia stood a bit taller under that proclamation. "I have a family now, and I owe you a debt for playing a part in it."

The woman's face fell a bit, and she cast a sidelong glance at Remus whose features were unreadable. "Yes, well, you're welcome."

Malia was dying to ask a dozen questions, but a familiar stench filled her nostrils, and without a word, she darted to Ellie's room. "Ellie, I'm back. We found it," she said excitedly.

The little girl coughed and rolled over. To Malia's horror, the child's skin had turned an ashy gray color, small blisters covered her skin, and the whites of her eyes were bloodshot and tear-filled. When she tried to speak, nothing came out for several seconds until Ellie was finally able to whisper with a gravelly voice, "I'm not going to make it."

"Yes, you will," Malia demanded.

It was Remus's voice who answered her, "No, my dear, she won't."

She spun around. "You are a god! Do something!"

"I'm a demigod, and even gods have limits, Malia."

She fisted her hands. "We brought you the samples. Everything you need should be in those bags."

"I understand that, and what we are looking for might be there, but we don't have time to search, to test it, to run experiments. Maybe, just maybe, if you'd found this weeks ago it would have worked, and we would have had the time to perfect it, but we are out of time. Ellie is dying. She's got minutes left."

"Then why bring all those people, why send us out one last time?"

"I didn't know she would turn so fast. The doctor is here to try to ease her pain; the others are people from my lab, they're taking the samples now."

"And the woman? Can't she do something?"

He cleared his throat. "Nova can ease her pain with her song when the medicine the doctor is using stops being effective."

Ellie tugged at Malia's sleeve. "I don't want to die, mom."

The words broke Malia's heart. She collapsed on the bed, scooping Ellie up in her arms and burying her face in her daughter's neck as they both sobbed. This child, who wasn't hers by blood or birth, was her entire world. She'd had too little time on this earth. Every child deserves to grow up, to outlive their parents, to fall in love, to know pain and joy, to have kids of their own. Ellie was being robbed of all of that. "I won't let you die, honey."

She blinked back her tears and picked Ellie up, walking slowly to the kitchen where the others were standing. She looked at all of them. "If any of you can save her, do it now."

One by one they all looked away. The siren showed her hand and glanced at Sam before she stepped back with the others who'd offered no help. Malia took a breath and turned to Sam. "Do it." He shook his head, and Malia cried, "Do it!"

Sam's heart dropped the moment Malia turned to him. Ellie lifted her weary head and stared at him pleading silently. Sam stepped forward and brushed Ellie's dark hair from her eyes. "The doctor can–"

Ellie shook her head. "Can you heal me?"

"No," he whispered back. It was the truth. As much as Malia stood there shaking her head in protest, and it broke his soul in two to deny either of them this, he couldn't do it. "I can't heal you."

Ellie looked from Malia to Sam and asked, "Then why does my mom think you can?"

"Because she was dying and I saved her."

"Then..." Ellie's words trailed off into a coughing fit.

"I can't heal, Ellie. I'm a ghoul; I turned Malia so that she wouldn't leave you all alone. She's a ghoul now."

Her little mouth opened in a silent O shape but no words came out. Malia stiffened, and Sam's worst nightmare came to life in his kitchen. "Turn her," his mate demanded.

Tears filled the little girl's eyes, and she reached for Sam. He held out his arms, and Malia let him take her. Her little voice whispered in his ear, "Does death hurt?"

Sam's head rested against hers. "I don't know; I was born this way."

"Ghoul's aren't dead?"

He gave a sad laugh. "No, we are living creatures."

"If I die, you won't leave again, will you?"

"No."

Remus cleared his throat and took Ellie from Sam, and in a stern voice Sam hadn't heard since his youth, Rem commanded, "You two leave the girl with me and go sort your shit out. She's got a limited amount of time." The unspoken words echoed in Sam's head. *'You can save her, make your choice.'*

Malia was already down the stairs and pacing; he could feel the anger rolling off of her in waves. As soon as he was near her, she spun on him and tossed him into a bookshelf. "Do it, Sam. Save her."

"You hated me for changing you. Do you really want that life for her?"

"Yes," she blurted out without a second thought. Her eyes changed red, and he watched as she flexed her clawed hands. Her voice grew low and cold, making the hairs on the back of his neck stand on end. "I will hate you if you let her die."

"Do you think I want that, Malia? I love that little girl; it's killing me to see her suffering, but there is no infection or disease to eat out of her, and if I change her, then we are condemning her to a life of being hunted. We don't have human lifespans; I'm considered young by our standards and Rem found me over ninety years ago. I was already a teenager then. You have to eat flesh to survive now. Do you want that for her?"

"She'll adapt. I'm sure she'll be able to eat it. How do other ghoul children manage? Whatever they do, she can do the same. And as for surviving, she's a fighter; she'll learn to hunt, not be the hunted. If you love her, then—"

He wrapped her in his arms, crushing her against her struggling. "From the moment we knew she wasn't going to get better I wanted to fix it for her, but this is a hard life. I already told you, I never wanted this life for any kid of mine."

"But—" Malia whispered through her tears. "Now?"

"You have no idea how much I want to turn her, make us a family, but what if what happened to my parents happens to us?"

"We have people who will protect her; she won't be alone like you were. Reagan and Remus will keep her safe if Bast comes for us." He blinked and pulled back from her. His brow drew together in a tight line. Malia touched his cheek and swallowed. "That's what you're afraid of, isn't it? You think he killed your parents so he could control our tribe, and you think that he will come after us and leave Ellie an orphan. Bast won't ever get close enough to hurt her. I promise. We're a family, Sam. She needs your strength. I need you." She swallowed again. "We will keep her safe, and we will surround her with others who will protect her."

"She'll be a monster," Sam's voice was so low he barely heard himself speak the words out loud.

Malia lifted his chin to meet his gaze. "You are not a monster, Samuel. You are the furthest thing from a monster. You saved us. You protected us. Why would you do that, if you are truly a monster?"

"Because I love you, both of you."

"Monsters don't love; they don't sacrifice everything for other people. You did that. You are a king, a loyal man, and I believe she is better off having a life with us than having no life at all."

The faint sound of coughing echoed from the apartment and Sam went rigid. He snapped his head towards the door and flexed his fingers. A part of him didn't know if he had the courage to do it. Another part of him wanted to believe

Malia when she said that they would protect Ellie, or at least make sure she was protected, if Bast came for them. He was bewildered as to how she picked up on his suspicions of Bast, but he had a feeling his mate's intuition might be a hand-me-down gift from her demigod grandfather. She slipped her hand into his and gave the slightest nod. "Save our daughter, Sam."

Malia's hair danced in the breeze left behind as Sam became a blur right before her eyes. One minute she was encouraging him and the next he was gone. She traversed the stairs, heart pounding in her chest and an ache filling her belly. He had a right to his fears. His fears of her hatred of him, she'd proven that one right the night he changed her and she told him she never wanted to see him again. His fears of leaving a child all alone in a cruel world. His fears of humans or the Agency hunting Ellie down. All valid, but something hummed inside her, some small voice that told her it would all be okay.

Ellie would have a full life; she would be the daughter of the Black King, and she would be protected by a great-grandfather who happened to be a demigod. She would have a witch mated to an alpha wolf and a full pack behind them to watch over her. And a siren who could sing her sleep into the sweetest dreams any little girl could possibly have. As she pushed open the door, all eyes fell on Malia, and she felt her heart stop for one brief second. Her eyes widened. "What happened? Is she okay?" Covering her mouth as everyone in the kitchen turned in unison towards the hallway, Malia slowly made her way to Ellie's room.

Her legs shook, the somber looks of the paranormal creatures filled her with dread. Her one hand still covered her mouth to hold back the bubbling sobs as she reached out her other hand to the cold wall for extra support. Only her will kept her feet moving forward when all she wanted to do was crumble. Something had gone wrong. Sam wasn't fast enough. They'd wasted too much time. Everything was lost. Her world that began to take shape the moment a strange woman died in a cargo container leaving behind a scared little girl and had morphed into a love Malia could barely contain was coming to an end.

She entered the room. Sam knelt next to the bed, Ellie laid on top of the blankets. Her chest didn't rise. Malia swallowed down the cry that wanted to come wrenching free from her lungs, and her legs gave out. As soon as she hit the floor, the tears and screams came. Strong arms wrapped her up, not having the strength to look up, she could tell by the scent that Sam was the one holding her. He was walking with her, carrying her the short distance to the bed and laid her down next to Ellie's body.

Malia squeezed her eyes tighter at the sound of Sam's voice. "Open your eyes, Malia."

She shook her head. Her sobs choked her, and she shook until a small, warm hand rested against her cheek. Malia froze. Her nostrils flared taking in the sweet smell of honey and lavender that filled the room. "Ellie?" Her eyes flew open, and Ellie laid in front of her. Bright eyes and a beaming smile greeted her.

The stench of death was gone, and the little girl's melodic voice danced in the air, "Don't cry, mom."

Malia grabbed Ellie's hand and pressed it against her lips. In her sickened state, she hadn't felt warm; her skin had been constantly cold and clammy. Now life radiated through her. Malia's sobs turned into a mix of laughter and tears as she pulled her daughter against her and held on to her for dear life. The bed depressed and Malia felt Sam's lips press against her forehead as he sat next to them.

Time stood still. She had no idea how long they stayed like that. The family she never expected to have. The daughter who meant more to her than life. And the man who gave up everything for them. Her tears finally exhausted themselves and she fell asleep wrapped up with the two most important people in her world.

CHAPTER TEN

"Mary has escaped the Agency with a bit of inside help." A hush fell over the tribe who'd gathered at the club for Sam's announcement.

Bast was the first to speak up, "Where is she?"

"She won't be returning." Sam held up his hand to quiet the mumble of voices. "Her return would put us all in jeopardy; she is safe and will be leaving the country. I have made arrangements for her overseas where she will live a nice and comfortable life."

The leader stood up and raised his voice, "That isn't your call to make. You don't lead us, Sam."

"It is my call to make. I am your king."

"By default. You've manipulated our queen, poisoned her against us. You are the great betrayer—"

Malia cocked her head and rose to her feet. "I am not the heir to this tribe—"

"You are," he interrupted.

She glared and continued, "I am not the direct descendant of Al-Malik al-Aswad." Turning to Sam, she held out her hand and smiled as he took it. "I wasn't born a ghoul. I was changed, and my maker is the Black King."

A hush fell over the crowd. A few darted their eyes to Bast while others began to bow their heads. Sam leaned over and kissed Malia's cheek as Ellie squeezed his hand. "I am your king." His eyes changed to emphasize his point.

The black mask of veins surrounding his black and red eyes made it clear to everyone in the room. In response, the ghouls who had bowed looked up, and Sam felt a swell of pride seeing their transformation. The whites of their eyes turned red, and the irises became white. He bowed to them in return and turned his attention back to Bast and the others. "You may stay, but if you have any objections to my leadership, then feel free to leave. This is your one chance. If you choose to stay, I expect loyalty, because war is coming and we need a united front."

Bast bristled. "We will not serve you. You are nothing but a puppet for Rem, and no human will ever pull our reins."

"Bast, you and I will have our reckoning one day, but I will not let you take our people down with you. No one pulls my strings. Not Rem, not you."

As Bast attempted to step closer, the tribe rose, blocking his path. "What are you all doing? You can't follow this fool. His parents' ideals almost ruined us before; he will do the same. It's time we took our place as rulers once more and subjected the humans to the same slavery they once bound us to."

Sam growled, "What are you talking about?"

Bast laughed. "You think we've been living a pure life, staying hidden in plain sight of the humans? You're naive. Your parents tried that utopia shit over a hundred years ago and look where it got them." A small group of men from the back of the club moved toward Bast; their eyes changed, and saliva dripped from the mouths. "We've been at war for longer than you think, Sam. Why do you think there are still so many stories about ghouls? We are the humans' worst nightmares. We are the reason they tell their children to be afraid of the monsters under the bed. You were stupid enough to believe that we all lived our lives with your moral standards, your way will get us nowhere."

The color drained from Sam's face; his people were killers. Monsters who murdered innocent people. And the only suspect he'd ever had in his parents' murder was standing here gloating about it. Fury blinded him, and Sam lunged. Blood sprayed the room, and before Bast could draw a breath, his body laid on the floor in a puddle of blood. Sam's shoulders shook, and he raised his head to meet the eyes of his tribe. "Anyone who followed Bast, this is your only warning," he bared his teeth and snapped, letting out a deep growl, "Run far and fast. When I find you, you will suffer. If I hear of a killing that sounds even remotely like a ghoul feeding, I will come for you. Hide, never take another human life again, and I will spare you."

The few men that had stood with Bast stared in horror at their leader's fallen body until Sam gave another growl, and all of them fled from the building. He was left with a slightly smaller crowd, but one that was loyal, and for that, he couldn't be more grateful. "Do you accept me as your king and my mate as your queen?"

One by one they all lowered to one knee with bowed heads. Sam looked down at Ellie and smiled, squeezing her small hand in his. "And do you accept my daughter as the heir to my throne?"

The group stood up. One man pulled a small silver knife from his belt and slid it across his palm, passing it off to the woman next to him. He stepped up, kneeling in front of Ellie and squeezed his hand until a drop of blood fell to the floor next to her feet. The rest of the group followed suit, and Ellie looked up at Sam. "What are they doing?"

He winked, still holding her hand. "They are pledging their life to you. You are their princess."

She grinned from ear to ear until the last person had finished the ritual. Then her smile faded, and she looked back up at him again. "And I have to eat people?"

He shook his head. "Not for a couple more years. You won't fully transform until you hit puberty. Don't worry; it's not as bad as it sounds."

She nodded, seeming satisfied with that answer. The door to the club opened, and Ellie squealed in excitement, "Grandpa!"

Remus embraced her as soon as she ran to him. Picking her up, he twirled her around and sat her back down. "You're looking well, sweet pea." She laughed and wrapped her arms around him. The look on Remus's face gave Sam the impression that the demigod wasn't quite used to having someone hug him, but he played along to the delight of Ellie.

Malia called out, "Ellie, come on. I think grandpa needs to talk to dad."

A moment later Sam found himself in Bast's old office staring in shock at Remus. "Excuse me? You want me to what?"

"Join the Syndicate. Sit at the table and represent your people. They deserve to have their voices heard. This will be your district; uptown will belong to the ghouls."

"I'm mated to your granddaughter, I now have a child to care for, and you want me to join the mafia?" Sam pinched the bridge of his nose. "Just what sort of illegal activity will the ghouls be in charge of?"

"The same activity that you already partake in. Surveillance from inside the human departments. Police, medical, legal, political. Your people have the inside gambit on this city, hell, you have the inside gambit worldwide, and one day you will rule over all of them once they are united. You are the Black King; your job is to rule them all, not just one tribe. And your access to inside information would be crucial to our organization."

Sam sat in the high-backed office chair and steepled his hands. "War is coming." Remus nodded. "And we will need allies." Remus nodded again. "The Agency will be hunting us."

This time Remus grinned. "Is that a yes?"

"Yes." He leaned back in the chair. "I'll do anything to protect my family and my people."

"Good." Remus set a piece of paper on the desk and turned to leave. "Be at that address tonight for a meeting. And I'm taking Bast's body with me. Consider it a gift. You won't have to clean up the mess."

Sam slid the paper into his pocket and waved as the door shut behind Remus. Malia and Ellie entered the room after a few minutes. Sam stood and looked around. "Well, what do you think? I suppose the club is now ours."

Malia shrugged. "I like the bookstore better."

He couldn't agree more. "Me too, but it is what it is."

Ellie jumped on the leather couch and laughed. "I like it here."

Sam scooped her up and spun her around before dropping her back on the couch. "Sorry, you don't get to hang out at the club. The bookstore is home."

Ellie stuck out her bottom lip and resumed her jumping as Malia wrapped her arms around Sam and whispered, "What did Remus want?"

"To ask me to join the Syndicate."

She stepped back. "And, what did you say?"

"I said yes." Confusion colored her expression, and he caressed her cheek. "We need allies against the Agency. The Syndicate is the lesser of two evils, and if I am a part of it, I can help control which way everything goes."

"Makes sense." She leaned up to kiss him softly. "Are we safe?"

"You both will always be safe. I swear it." His mouth met hers sending a spark of heat arching between them. "I will lay down my life for both of you."

"And I you, my king."

The soft growl she made against his ear as she responded made every muscle in his body harden and coil. "It won't ever come to that," he promised, then nipped playfully at her earlobe. "Let's go home; I think we have a lot of time apart to make up for." Lowering his mouth to her ear he swirled his tongue over the part of her ear he'd just teased with his teeth and whispered, "My queen."

CHAPTER ELEVEN

Nova's heels clicked against the cold stone floor of the warehouse. "Remus, what do you plan to do with him?"

The demigod looked up and gave the siren a heated once over and smiled. "Teach him a lesson."

She sighed and placed her hands on her hips. "He was almost dead; Sam practically decapitated him. Don't you think the Black King would like to know this piece of filth is still alive?"

Remus cracked his knuckles and stepped up to examine Bast's bloody body. The treacherous ghoul was hanging by his wrists, his feet barely skimming the floor where a pool of blood had formed from Remus's rounds of interrogation. The demigod chucked the ghoul under the chin and spat. "I was friends with Sayyid and Naomi Jinn." He turned to Nova and cocked his head. "Did you know that?" When she shook her head, he added, "I am Sam's godfather, and he has no idea. Funny, isn't it?"

Nova stilled, and he knew she was planning her next words carefully. "Did you know what would happen to Malia?"

His swirling eyes gleamed. "I've known for decades that Sam would rise up to take his parents' place. I knew he would play an important role in my life. And in a way, I knew what would happen to Malia."

"In a way?"

"I knew she wouldn't survive. Her time on this earth was limited, and without some intervention, my bloodline would end."

"How did you know that?"

His lips twitched into a menacing smile. "A little spy told me."

"Lisa?" Nova asked.

Remus shook his head. "No, though she was the one who informed me about my blood connection with Malia and pointed me in the right direction. But another Agency asset gave me the information that had me lining up my chess pieces for this round. She's the one that saw Malia's life ending." He shrugged. "I couldn't allow that. I couldn't let Romulus take her away from Sam or me."

Bast made a grumbling sound, and Remus grabbed a red-hot poker from a nearby burn barrel. "You wanted to know what I planned to do with this ghoul?" He poked the red tip of the metal into Bast's side and grinned as the ghoul shouted and thrashed in pain. "I don't think you want to stick around to see, my dear."

"I think you're right, Remus."

He took notice of the sway of her hips as she made her way to the exit. Sirens were always a welcome distraction from business. Before she could leave Remus called out, "Be a lamb, my dear, and bring in my chainsaw and the roll of plastic from my trunk." He tossed her his keys and grinned. "Just leave them by the door, I'll make sure to clean up after myself."

He could feel the tension building around Nova's aura, but she knew the score. None of them had clean hands in this life. Him least of all. He might be better than Romulus, but they were both different sides of the same coin. He would do what it took to win; his brother would do the same. Remus would kill, torture, maim, and spy same as Romulus, but the lines drawn in the sand were what separated them. Remus had no qualms about what was about to go down with Bast. The man was a traitor to his kind, a thief of power he had no right to claim, and a cold-blooded killer of innocent humans, children, and dearly departed friends. Romulus used his drug to kill indiscriminately. He had his people testing its effects on the young and old alike. The Agency had poisoned Ellie simply for the purpose of recording how long it might take to kill someone with much smaller and diluted doses.

What they'd done to Malia, abducting her to sell her into slavery, and what they'd done to Ellie, trying to poison a child, were lines Remus and his Syndicate would never cross. If the Syndicate came for you, there was a reason. If the Agency came, it was a whole other story. He made his way to the door after Nova dropped off the items. He picked up the chainsaw and started it. Bast flinched and squirmed against his binding. Remus grinned. "Let's have some fun, Bastiel Jinn. The horrors you visited upon your own brother and his mate will be nothing compared to my vengeance."

His prisoner screamed and struggled against his binding, but it was the sheer look of terror when Bast met Remus's eyes that made the demigod smile. Bast stuttered "Your—Your eyes..."

Remus's body vibrated with rage and hatred, but he did enjoy watching Bast's fear grow. His lips twitched and pulled back into a menacing grin. Bastiel's fear was sustenance to the darkest parts of Remus's soul, and nowadays it rarely got fed. His swirling eyes had stopped their hypnotic dance and glowed silver. Revving the chainsaw again, he worked slowly. This was pleasure, revenge, and justice, and Remus planned to take his time. He'd worry about the mess later.

As Peterson hung up the phone and frowned, Jake sat up a little straighter. "Well? What was that all about?"

The wolf picked up a pencil and tapped it on his desk. "There's a raging fire at one of the addresses we sent to Reagan. Looks like the Agency is trying to cover their tracks."

"Arson?" Jake leaned closer. "Are you sure?"

"The investigator won't be able to get in there until they get the fire put out, but yeah, that'd be my guess."

"Gut instinct?" the vampire teased.

Peterson laughed. "Yep, because we both know nothing happens around here by coincidence."

"True." Jake adjusted his holster and leaned back in his chair. "So where does that leave us?"

"Nowhere. Fire isn't our department. We leave it up to whoever they give the case to, but we need to clean our records and make sure no one can trace those addresses to our internal searches."

"Right." Jake hopped to his feet. "I'll get ahold of Skye and have her do a clean sweep." He paused at the door. "Any idea who this Specimen 21 is?"

"Nope, but whoever he or she is we need to find them and figure out how they fit into this whole mess."

"Great, sound like fun," he quipped. "Note my sarcasm."

"Duly noted." Peterson laughed. "Get to work, Special Agent Rosenthal, after this we have a ghoul king to meet up with. Remus says this Samuel Jinn will have a seat at the table, and his new district should yield some very valuable information for the Syndicate."

Jake narrowed his eyes. "You do remember that I'm not a part of your little mafia club, right?"

Peterson barked a laugh. "Oh, I remember. I just choose to ignore your stubbornness in the matter, partner. Now, hurry up. We have a king to meet."

"What about the Unity Rally? Aren't we supposed to be preparing for that?" Jake leaned against the door and met Peterson's gaze. "I thought every available agent was being assigned to keep the peace between the supporters and the protesters."

A line of concern creased Peterson's forehead. "The rally's been postponed; tensions are too high right now. The humans who support unity are on shaky ground with the current wave of crime tarnishing their hopes of bringing everyone together; which is whipping the protestors into a frenzy. The world is a powder keg right now, any little spark and we all go up in flames."

As he turned back to the door, Jake muttered, "Too bad. We could all use a little unity right now."

"Ain't that the truth," Peterson replied as he gathered up his jacket. "I'll meet you in the parking garage; we don't want to keep the Black King waiting."

ABOUT THE AUTHORS

A.L. KESSLER

A.L. Kessler is the author of the best-selling series Here Witchy Witchy. She resides in Colorado with her family and pets. Her addiction to coffee and chocolate fuels her creativity to bring her readers wonderful stories. Learn more at www. amylkessler.com

CONNECT WITH HER ONLINE:
Website: http://www.amylkessler.com
Facebook: https://www.facebook.com/alkesslerauthor
Twitter: https://twitter.com/A_L_Kessler
Google+: https://plus.google.com
Goodreads: http://www.goodreads.com/author/show/6548820.A_L_Kessler

OTHER SERIES BY A.L. KESSLER
Here Witchy Witchy
Dark War Chronicles
Children of the Apocalypse

Want to know a secret? Scan the QR code or follow the link
http://bit.ly/ALkesslerroom

MIA BISHOP

Mia Bishop lives in Colorado with her husband, two boys, and enough animals to fill a mini-zoo. She writes to keep from dying of boredom in the high desert. Mia loves to write paranormal romance and erotica, but also enjoys the steampunk and post-apocalyptic genres as well as historical romances.

A geek at heart, Mia indulges in all matters of nerd cultures. When not writing, she can be found with her nose in a book or graphic novel, watching anime, playing video games, or creating pieces of chainmail and wire jewelry. The key to Mia's heart can be won with anything Whovian related, tickets to ComicCon, or a '67 black Chevy Impala.

You can follow Mia at links below:
Newsletter: http://bit.ly/2aytKPc
Blog: http://bit.ly/1dzTwuK
Facebook Page: http://on.fb.me/M1FxZq
Twitter: http://bit.ly/1dZUlBG
Google+: http://bit.ly/1eIm6xW
Tumblr: http://goo.gl/dRhfsy
Goodreads: http://bit.ly/1l3taeD
Amazon: http://amzn.to/1mVlgoC
Instagram: http://bit.ly/1fo4J3F

OTHER BOOKS BY MIA BISHOP

Waking Up In Bedlam

Ryder is a fake- and he knows it. He spends his days pretending to be a paranormal investigator and his nights entertaining groups of believers with his claims of communicating with the dead. Life is good and business is booming until the night a beautiful woman storms out of his seminar and a mysterious man drops an unexplainable case in his lap. Ryder finds out the world he thought was fake is actually real and even worse, he has become the paranormal world's most wanted.
Jessa wants answers and the human, Ryder, is the only one who can give them to her. She has one goal, keep him alive long enough to figure out why he has been haunting her dreams. The only problem is the more time she spends with him the more she realizes the answers she seeks are ones she isn't ready to face.
Can either one of them accept what fate has laid out for them? Or will they fight their destiny at the cost of everyone they hold dear?

Amazon: http://amzn.to/1cBuIT2

*Sacrifice_*

In the New Mexico desert evil is stirring. A lost man must protect everything he holds dear from the oncoming storm and a mysterious woman is the key.
A decade after being forced out of the priesthood, Nico Lynch spends his days drinking himself into an early grave and his nights hunting demons. His world is turned upside down when he is asked to help a local Striga Coven.
Abby shouldn't have survived, but she did and that's turning out to be one hell of a problem for Nico. The world he lives in is black and white. There has always been a clear definition between good and evil, right and wrong. Every moment he spends with Abby challenges him to see the world differently.
Mysterious forces have brought them together, pitting them against a demon army. Nico will either be the savior of mankind or the catalyst of the apocalypse and Abby's fate rests in his hands.

Amazon: http://amzn.to/2a5mA7l

Blood & Ink Press thanks you for supporting indie authors "The more that you read, the more things you will know. The more that you learn, the more places you'll go." -Dr. Seuss

Follow us to find your next destination: Blood & Ink Press Dark and Wicked Fiction https://www.facebook.com/bloodinkpress/
https://bloodandink.com

BLOOD & INK PRESS

Printed in Great Britain
by Amazon